# Writing in the Q

ROBERT GRANADER

ISBN: 978-1-62429-379-5

Published through Opus Self-Publishing
Politics and Prose Bookstore
5015 Connecticut Ave. NW
Washington, D.C. 20008
www.politics-prose.com / / (202) 364-191

# Table of Contents

Introduction                                             3

A Parking Lot in the Q                                   5

The Kippah Drawer                                       12

Curable                                                 23

Camping Alone with Nick                                 39

Girl on the Balcony                                     50

Counting Heads                                          58

No Upside                                               67

The Rise of the Parking Lot                             75

The Secret Lives of Parking Lots                        78

The Rabbi's Story                                       81

Chargeback                                              91

Talking Windows                                        101

Winning Numbers                                        111

She Said Yes                                           123

A Pain Called Laura                                    126

Blog and Business Writing                              129

    Shrinking Turkeys, Expanding Markets            131

    What's Your Story? And How To Lead With It      134

    Next Year's Trends Are Already Here             138

    PPP a Chance to Pause, Plan and Pivot           142

So Who Are We Now? Remote Work
and Its Impact on Company Culture                               145

Personal Blogs: In a Foreign Land                              148

Whither the Handshake?                                         152

Graduation Cancelled, Life Postponed, the Kids are Alright    155

Returning Bugs                                                 161

## Conclusion                                                  165

# Writing in the Q

ROBERT GRANADER

# Introduction

ALL THESE STORIES WERE WRITTEN OR PUBLISHED DURING THE MAIN part of the Covid-19 Pandemic: March 2020-Fall 2021. I also added some personal as well as professional blogs to round out the sense of what it was like during this epochal moment.

It goes without saying that writing is a solitary endeavor. But story ideation often comes from very public places. Covid magnified this, in-part because coffee shops and other gathering places where writers seek distanced-companionship, were off limits. So many stories spring from our everyday interactions and those were curtailed.

In a few places I quote Gabriel Garcia Marquez when he said: "All human beings have three lives: public, private, and secret."

Writers often find their ideas in public and then run them through the private and the secret. Much was lost.

Most of these stories come from a primal need to express ourselves during this period where it feels like Atlas shrugged. A time when young adults were back home, when the offices went empty, and Starbucks delivered espresso at the curb. In "A Sense of Where You Are," John McPhee writes about Bill Bradley and his sense of always knowing where the basket was when he was on the court. Writing is often my roadmap to understanding and remembering.

Admittedly we had it pretty easy. I can't imagine the challenges of living alone or having to care for small children or homeschooling a middle schooler. I felt bad for our son having to teach his students on Zoom from his childhood bedroom, when he knew they were more likely to ask for help without everyone else listening. Watching them cancel our daughter's college graduation, her first job stunted by quarantine, unable to get mentored in person, meet co-workers for a drink or go to an office. And college for our youngest was disrupted in Sophomore year by Covid, in Junior year by mask mandates and then Hurricane Ida and the Delta variant shook up Senior year.

But there was growth and progress and thankfully, quiet moments where a story started or was completed or finally accepted.

Living in quarantine (the Q) was unique. This is a first draft of how it was.

# A Parking Lot in the Q

*I lead with this story because it encapsulates so much about writing and living during the pandemic, the sense of changing course, of being surprised, of thinking differently.*

*This story popped into my head as an essay about the rise of the parking lot (that essay can be found deeper in the book). It then morphed into a story and as I wrote I asked more questions and wondered what the story was trying to say.*

*At first it was a straightforward story about a guy walking and noticing, but nothing happened. So I added the quirky ending. It received a very positive response from editors, and four acceptances, so I started putting quirky twists and more imaginative characters throughout my stories, with some success.*

*In October of 2020 Adam Davis of the* Green Hills Literary Lantern *wrote in the opening line of his acceptance: "Thanks for letting us see this odd piece."*

*"Odd" seemed to sell during Covid.*

*Other takers included* Brushfire, Meadow *and the* Penmen Review.

*"Everyone has three lives: a public life, a private life and a secret life."*
—G.G. Marquez

THE CARS HAVE PEOPLE IN THEM.

It takes me awhile to realize this, but after a few weeks in the Q, as the kids call it, I notice everything. Everything I used to miss. The people who live in this neighborhood of mine, a place that had been the equivalent of flyover country.

The places you don't notice because they are in between destinations.

5

But the people in these parked cars don't notice me, on purpose I presume. Why are they filling up the lot of this deserted school? Their eyes are plugged in to their phones or staring at a tree off in the distance. Their cars are shut, the engines run.

The parking lot is near my house, just behind a school. The school has a normal name, not a religious one, yet Mother Mary and Jesus hang from its walls.

Maybe they are here to pray?

I used to walk this path after dinner with my wife just us and the two yappy dogs. We would talk about our day. That was before the Q, when we'd spend our free time together. Now we are both home and I feel the need to leave. I don't think she notices.

Early in the morning when the sun is just coming up I leave with the dogs and walk the lot. As the Q lingers I find myself getting out no matter the weather.

At night we take the same path. But at night it is quiet, just other dog walkers, barkers and droopy-faced pups, people with masks, a tennis ball ping pong-ing off a racket in the distance, cars going the speed limit. Everything is slower and the lot is clean of cars.

But during the day when I am alone the parking lot is ablaze, buzzing with muted activity within hermetically sealed cars. Lots of them, some slotted in their spots, some parked askew as if to say, "just visiting," parked like they are curb-side waiting for a pizza pick-up.

On other days they are parked one space apart like men at a row of urinals.

There are the regulars and I have private nicknames for them all:

—Folgers Man rests his steaming coffee cup on the back of his flatbed, staring out at the empty soccer field as if he were being filmed for a Folgers ad.

—The Grunter grunts a few cars down three times a week, a woman parks her car between two white lines, a yoga mat and weights fill up the other spot as she squats and stretches, pushes and pulls, oblivious to the dog walker.

—Mad Man sits in his two-seat convertible reads a newspaper while sucking on a cigarette.

—White vans with ladders on top waiting for a job

—The Company Man paces in a blue vest with a company logo on the breast. On calls every day, just pacing, pacing, pacing.

—Uber-looking cars waiting for food orders.

In between these pods the dog-walkers stroll, the bike-riders slalom, a man pulls two kids in a red plastic Radio Flyer and parents grab their children as engines fire up.

To me they are just silhouettes — quiet, un-emotional and distant. But as the quarantine lingers so do they. They settle in and turn off their cars, their windows come down and their world opens up, to me.

Their voices echo off the doors in the morning stillness, their stories become clearer as I hear one, then another and another. The conversations are not a crowd-like mush of white noise, but more distinct. It's a large dinner table with *new* friends, where you can hear whoever you focus on.

With each step I hear pieces of confessions, pleas and cries.

"I can talk," I hear someone say, his tone sympathetic.

I want to stop and hear the rest of the story, but I feel compelled to act like I can't hear him. Like I'm not eavesdropping. So I keep walking. I am embarrassed, not for me, but for them. Why don't I want to be seen? I'm the one just walking, they are the ones doing something in whispered tones.

So I tip toe through the lot looking at my dogs, adjusting my phone to appear busy by scrolling.

I try to puzzle it together, but I hear only secrets that don't fit.

"I am listening" a woman says in a way that makes me think she means it, but that the person on the end thinks she doesn't.

"I just had to get out."

"It's gonna be okay."

"Does it make you happy?"

"I can't take much more of this."

They are mask-less in their cars yet I don't recognize anybody, except a man in the Black BMW. There is a familiarity to him. I think it's the same car I once drove? I walk past and try to look through the glare of his windshield, but I only hear fragments from his phone:

"He just left," a woman says. Her voice is familiar, it sounds like so many voices I've heard on speaker phones. The words echo in a tinny vibration. When she finishes he quickly drives off.

If everyone has three lives, as Marquez said, then these are their secret lives. They are here for the relationship now relegated to phone calls, the conversations they hope vanish into the ether, the release they cannot get in a house full of unattended kids. I see a man swallow cheese whiz straight from the can, a drunk woman swigs Coca Cola out of the bottle. A woman eats ice cream from the carton without taking it out of the plastic grocery bag, and a man drinks small bottles of alcohol that he tosses into the woods when he thinks no one is looking.

At night when we walk the same steps through the empty lot I don't tell Katie about what I've found during the day, this waiting room to somewhere. I don't share with her the fragments of the lives of our neighbors who are killing time or taking meetings or making deals with themselves about the time they need, validating this world they created.

Maybe it's not so different. Before the pandemic we talked about our day but did I tell her everything? Did she tell me all the times she thought about something I would want to know?

I don't tell her how the parking lot near our home has become a soccer field, a bicycle track, a workout room, a coffee house, a diner, a back porch, a dog park, a phone booth, a bar, a rec room, an office park, a confessional, a synagogue, a hotel room, a movie theatre, a lunch counter, a drive-in. It's a place where people act like no one is watching.

She would think it weird that I've created this place. But I would argue I've only discovered it. Others likely walk through the lot or toward the soccer field and never notice the people inside these cars. The ones I've become so curious about. The ones who keep me up at night wondering whether everyone has a secret life and what do they do about it?

I feel like the man in the BMW recognizes me too. I'm not good with names, I must know him, I just can't place him.

In all the weeks of walking I only ever spoke with one person, or rather he spoke to me. I'd seen him before, the hood-leaner. He was never in his car, always on a call, resting his elbows on the hood and smiling. Not a crazy smile, but a welcoming one, he was trying to make eye contact, I could feel it the way you can tell with some people that they are trying to interact.

"You must live around here," he said in a friendly tone, pulling a pod from his ear. "You like my office?"

No one had even made eye contact let alone spoken to me in all these months and all these laps. I felt oddly safe behind my mask. Startled I pulled out my own earpiece, "yea, I live just a few blocks away." It was reflexive, I have no idea why I told him anything.

I stopped to let the dogs sniff his flip flops

"I can't work at home," he tells me without prompting.

I say nothing unable to get my bearings with this guy.

"I go out to the field with some golf balls and work on my chipping in between calls," he said.

I nod and yank at the dog's leash.

We never speak again.

After weeks of seeing the same people I am now convinced I know them, wondering anew if I know them from someplace else. Like Black BMW.

But I don't reach out to him or any of them. It's their time to stare into a bank of trees, or the brick wall that surely makes up one side of the empty school gym. I don't want them telling me their stories, I want to hear them, without editorial. They are here to live the life they can't live anywhere else. All the things they did before the quarantine when the kids were at school, when they had a private office, when they had to commute.

Their public lives are filtered through Zoom.

Their private lives are confined within the walls of our homes.

But their secret lives are the ones that have been edited out by the quarantine.

There are still secrets, they are just housed in a parking lot outside a school.

I want to know how their stories end? Where do they go next? What lie are they telling someone when they come home?

As the reins of the Pandemic loosen I venture outside my neighborhood and I search the crowds for my people from the lot. The relationship is one-sided, I hide behind a mask, they sit behind a windshield.

All these people live within a football field of my house and yet there's not a hint of recognition? As hard as I try to place them my only real memories are from the lot.

"Aren't you going?" Katie asks me one morning from the other side of the bed.

"Going where?"

"The dogs. The vet?" she reminded me.

I was tired, but she was right.

"Looks like rain," I said as I shuffled to the bathroom to brush my teeth.

The dogs started jumping at the sight of their leashes. I tried to explain to them that we weren't going for a walk. But we went outside to the car and they pulled me toward the park. There was still time and besides it was Tuesday and I wanted to see the Grunter and her yoga mat.

We began the usual route and one of the dogs pulled me to the lot, but the other toward home, perhaps sensing the rain that was to come.

As the first drops hit the back of my neck my head swiveled as the black BMW pulled past me. I hurried the dogs along as the rain began falling. As I rounded the corner of my street I could see my wife on the front porch waving the Black BMW up the driveway. The man emerged from his car, pulled up his jacket to hide from the rain as my wife ushered him inside.

# The Kippah Drawer

*This story remains tops for its wide appeal as it was accepted by* JewishFiction.net, Headway Quarterly *and* Magnolia Review *(which reprinted it). There was also a story written about it in the* Detroit Jewish News *by a guy who liked the story enough to write a short essay about it. I've thought about expanding this story or converting it to the stage, there is more here.*

*The one hitch I had was a discussion with an editor who wanted me to drop the "h" at the end of Kippah and Challah, saying it is more accepted now without the h. I am willing to use only one space after a period, but I wouldn't drop the dangling h.*

THE DRAWER WAS STUFFED.

When he tugged at the wooden knob, a fluff of velvet and satin bulged out. It always happened when he opened this drawer, one of only two drawers in his small dining room. He never emptied it. He'd only overstuff it, which required him to kneel down, his eighty-nine-year-old knees crackling like dry twigs as he picked up the escaped yarmulkes, kissing them gently before packing them back in the drawer.

Except for the one he had on his head for that evening.

Yossi lived alone and only wore his yarmulke on the Sabbath, but his drawer runneth over with not one or two or three of these skullcaps worn by Jews to show their reverence for God. He had dozens upon dozens, his drawer a time machine of simchas, happy occasions.

There were nights, now more than before, when he couldn't sleep. He'd been alone for so long, but he had felt it more keenly in the past year. He wasn't sure why. Perhaps it was his bladder, waking him in the middle of night, now frightening him in some way. Or maybe that large bed that he once shared with his wife was getting bigger as he got smaller, and so when his leg stretched to the vast emptiness on the other side, the chill from the untouched sheets would startle him and jerk him awake.

On these nights he would lie there hoping, praying, that he would fall back to sleep. When it did not happen, he'd get out of bed and tread the cold floor of his apartment to the drawer. And with the thin light that hung above, he'd dive his hand into the drawer and swim it around as if he were picking out a raffle ticket. He'd open a yarmulke and hold it up to the light, stretching his arm and pulling it close to read the names and dates of the people imprinted on the inside.

There was only one that needed no reminding. One navy blue kippah with gold trim and the date June 26, 1950. It was the lone remaining artifact from his wedding day. It was the one he wore most often and the one he could find, by feel, in the dark.

When a Jewish child turns thirteen, the family buys a set of one hundred kippot and imprints them with the name and date of the event. Every time a Jewish couple gets married, another hundred or so get printed. Sometimes Yossi wondered why he didn't go into the kippah business instead of accounting. Some guests would take the head coverings and wear them for the service, others dropped them in a box outside the sanctuary when the service was over, and some never picked them up. Still others, at the end of the service, absently left them on their heads or stuffed them in pockets to be found the next time they put on a suit.

Yarmulkes come in many flavors. Soft knit ones that only stay on with a clip. Others are velvet, hemmed with a lace border, grabbing the head whether covered in hair or freshly shaven.

And while Yossi and Malka never had children, thereby never having the extra seventy-five or so yarmulkes from a simcha of their own, he had not missed a Shabbat service in fifty years. He had seen hundreds of bnai mitzvot as boys and girls walked across the bima and made their case for being an adult in the eyes of the Jewish people. He'd pocketed dozens from weddings.

So each week as the guests filed out of the sanctuary for the free food, sweet wine and small cakes on doilies, he'd put a skullcap in his coat pocket.

And his collection grew.

"This is what you decided to collect?" Malka said one night as he filled the drawer. "Fabergé eggs wouldn't work?"

But for him the collection was a symbol of many things: his Judaism, his friendships, his years. For Yossi the filled drawer was like a collection of mitzvot, of good deeds, that built on itself over his life. This was the physical manifestation of all those prayers which made his life worthwhile.

"How do your fancy friends measure their worth?" he'd once asked Malka after a service where the bar mitzvah "theme" was some kind of video game. "Do they know how ludicrous they look standing in the sanctuary dressed as a Martian making Star Wars puns? Are they proud that their grandfather can't get through the Hamotzi without notecards?"

"Their assets, is that the measure? Their bank accounts, their houses? The vacations, the deals from long ago? They don't tell their story," he'd said.

They couldn't go into a dark room and watch the movie of their lives in a way that was as fulfilling as sitting on the floor recalling all the days of his life in synagogue. Maybe others had some ledger of good deeds, but for Yossi there was his drawer. It wasn't just that he'd attended all these events, but they represented days he'd spent in prayer, words he'd chanted over hundreds of hours of ancient texts. This was a visual representation of all he'd done.

"But none of them are ours," Malka would say.

"They are all ours," he said. "We've been to every one of these."

"We didn't matter," she said.

"Without us maybe they wouldn't have had a minyan," he said.

When they were younger Yossi and Malka would invite friends to their Friday night table. Malka would prepare the same dishes her mother had cooked from some recipe brought from the old country, scrawled on small slips of paper and stuffed into notebooks. And Yossi would pass out kippot to his guests, trying to find ones that might interest them. He'd find the wedding of a mutual friend or the bar mitzvah of a child they once knew. He wasn't sure if people ever noticed this planned coincidence, but sometimes it made for good conversation. Occasionally guests would walk away with a kippah by accident; it was the only time his drawer ever got smaller.

But inevitably he'd find these guests and remind them that he wanted the kippah back.

Now Yossi stood at the synagogue Shabbat table with his thimble of Manischewitz wine, looking at the faces, as he had for years. He and his friends used to congregate near one end of the

15

long, sweets-filled table. They would edge out the children who reached for handfuls of cakes.

But slowly his group dwindled. Yoni stopped coming when his wife got sick. Isaac had been missing since he fell six months ago. Moe had stopped driving. But most of them just died.

And now he'd go to the end of the table, less interested in pushing the kids out of the way. He felt the distance from everybody, even the rabbi, who would come over and shake his hand, saying, "Good Shabbos." But it was the new rabbi, not the one he knew for all the years. Not the one who buried Malka. He referred to this new rabbi, who always looked past him, spending more time with the people whose names graced the building's walls, as the CEO of the synagogue.

Yossi looked down at the carpet between his feet and the long, white tablecloth, remembering the mark his friends had left. The big, faded stains from where his friends had spilled wine or crumbled a cookie under their feet, or where frosting was driven into the carpet. There was nobody left in the room to remember these men who built this synagogue not with their money but with their attendance. And one day they would replace the carpet or get new linens, and there literally would be no sign left of the people who stood in these places for all those Saturday mornings.

At the other end of the table, away from the wine, was a group of kids, friends of the bar mitzvah boy, all with matching yellow corduroy yarmulkes, the ones that the family had given out that morning. And they were dropping them on the floor without kissing them, spilling grape juice on them. One used it as a napkin to wipe the frosting from his mouth.

And it was at this moment that he knew it was time. He knew those kids would never have a drawer because they didn't understand the power of ritual, the respect of the velvet, corduroy, or knitted, cloth.

And so he put his small cup down and walked to where the boys were roughhousing. They stopped when this old man stood in the middle of their pushing. Yossi knelt before them picking the yarmulkes off the floor, kissing them and placing them on their heads. But there were six boys and only five kippot. So he reached into his inside pocket and took an extra one he had brought, and gently planted it on a boy's head.

The boys said nothing, then slowly walked away, but not before grabbing another piece of cake.

Later that day as he ate his lunch alone at home, Yossi reached for his kippah, but it wasn't on his head. It was June 26th, and he was looking for the blue one with gold trim. His own private anniversary celebration. He reached into his pockets, then looked at his drawer, but nothing. His chest tightened, he grabbed his glasses and looked again, tilting his head to one side then another to let the light pass him by and illuminate the darkened corners of the drawer. But it wasn't there.

The sweat formed on his forehead and dripped into his eyes. He got up, a bit too quickly, banging his head on the opened cabinet. He reached for his head and couldn't tell if it was sweat or blood, but he didn't look. He hurried to his room, thrusting his hands into his jacket pockets, first one, then the next. It wasn't there.

He feared that in his moment of generosity he had given it away. He grabbed his tallis bag from the counter, and there he found the kippah.

Yossi went to the bathroom to check on his forehead and the damage he may have done.

Late that night he couldn't sleep and found himself on the floor in front of the kippah drawer. He dug down to the bottom and played with the oldest ones. He opened them slowly as some had not seen light in years. He realized that most of the kippot were of people he no longer knew or who had died some time ago. He remembered not so much the specific event, as they all ran into each other after a while, but his memory and these mementos of his friends and the couples who used to grace his Shabbat table were all he had. The only thing he had to spark their memory was this piece of cloth resting at the bottom of his darkened drawer.

These were his photo albums, his home movies, all waiting just for him. What a waste to sit in the dark for all these years. He realized that one of the only things that would spark a memory of him, or of Malka, might be this blue kippah he held in his hand.

It was time to empty the drawer.

It wasn't sad thoughts that drove him to this decision. It wasn't the empty bed or the quiet Shabbat table. There was no diagnosis, no threat, external or internal. It didn't happen in a doctor's office or a hospital waiting room. Standing over this drawer he found the strength to dispose of his one remaining asset.

And so he set out to give away a kippah a week. But his small synagogue didn't have enough events. It would take him years, which he knew he didn't have.

Each week *The Jewish News* arrived at his apartment, and he'd find the announcements, and then he would show up, whether he knew the family or not. And then he would plant a kippah on the heads where they were needed.

He no longer went with one extra kippah in his pocket. Now he walked around, his pockets full.

As usual he would show up early, find a seat, especially in these unfamiliar synagogues, participate in the service, watch the ceremony — the baby naming, the bar or bat mitzvah — and maybe stand and say Kaddish for somebody, for anybody who had nobody saying Kaddish for them. And then he would wait for his chance.

Yossi was content being there, "in the bleachers," as he would say, apart from it all. Happy not being the "entertainment." But when Malka was alive and they would attend events, it always bothered her.

"I don't like being part of the chorus," she would say. He had no interest in being center stage. The stress of pleasing all these people, the expectations were too much for him. He never understood why it was important for her to mingle with these fancy people who turned sacred services into social events.

So instead they would go to the service but leave before the Kiddish or the reception. Yossi felt disconnected from this world, but for Malka, during the three hours of the service, she felt like she was one of them. And isn't that what these special occasions were meant to do? To make you believe you are who you want to be? So in shul she wanted to be them,and could be. He didn't possess the power to fool himself.

But now, all alone, he was a guest of the best. He was at the biggest ceremonies and sometimes even stayed for the most lavish parties, mingling at the buffet, walking through the ballroom with a glass of red wine, a handful of chalah he'd pulled from the middle of the loaf.

No one questioned the old man in the dark suit. He knew it would have made Malka happy as he walked the floor, his wedding kippah on his head.

And he'd look for his opening, finding a boy with his head uncovered. Yossi would grab a kippah from his pocket, kiss it, and place it there.

For months he would go to events to which he wasn't invited, landing kippot on the heads of unsuspecting children. He did not know where these kippot would end up, who would drop them on the floor, who would let them fly off their heads in the parking lot. But there were some young men in that group who might reach for them one time, or see them in the mirror when they went to the bathroom that night, maybe even put them in a drawer in their home as a reminder of an event they'd never attended. These kippot were less time machine than eternal life. As long as someone wore that kippah and saw the names inscribed, then those names mattered. Week after week Yossi would dispense the kippot around town at every event where he could find a barren head. All throughout the summer and fall, and into the winter, he followed this pattern as his drawer emptied. Soon he could open the drawer without anything jumping out, and finally he was digging around the bottom finding old, faded ones.

On Friday nights he would open the drawer and decide which ones he'd give away the following day. In some way he was saying goodbye to these old friends before he sent them to a new head, perhaps a different house and an empty drawer.

The morning after he got the diagnosis, he stuffed into his pockets all the kippot that were left. Into the pants pocket, the outside jacket pocket, the inside pocket on each side, and he put the blue one on his head for the last time. He walked a little faster than usual, and maybe a little faster than a man his age should, that morning.

The Beckendorfs were having a bar mitzvah. When he arrived he saw a spread of lavender kippot on a wicker plate. Yossi took the plate and shook out all the lavender kippot into the wooden bin by the door. And then with great care he took the remaining kippot from his pockets, looking at each name before he lay its kippah on the tray.

Eternal life, he thought — that's what he was giving these long-forgotten members and their moment in time before iPhones and Snap stories recorded everything, when the only memories were in the minds of the people, most of whom were gone. But now someone might take these kippot with them and perhaps read the name and at least ask the question: Who were these people on these dates so long ago?

Yossi sat in the back and could feel his heart grow as he watched the rows of children, their heads covered with the random kippot from his drawer.

When the service ended Yossi made his way to the Kiddish, but not before stopping at the wooden bin to take for himself one of the lavender kippot the Beckendorfs had so carefully chosen.

Instead of standing in his usual spot, away from the partygoers, Yossi stood amid the bar mitzvah boy and his friends.

The young boy who was now a man stumbled, tripping over one of his friend's feet, his lavender kippah frisbeeing to the floor. The boy reached down, but Yossi was faster.

"Let me help you," Yossi said. And with one move Yossi placed a blue velvet kippah with gold trim on the boy's head. He held it there in place for a moment and closed his eyes.

The young man looked up at the old man but said nothing.

"Thank you," Yossi said.

And the boy ran off, one hand holding the kippah in place.

# Curable

*This was the first story published during Covid, though it was written late in 2019. This is not a sad story, instead it is about people trying to understand independence and what happens after we die. The* Evening Street Review *published it in March 2020 at the very start of the pandemic.*

I DON'T FEAR DYING. OR AT LEAST NOT THE WAY OTHERS DO.

I don't worry about missing my daughter's wedding or holding my grandchildren. I can see the next decade of empty-nest hood as days piled on top of weeks trying to fill the empty hours I'd accumulated over the years like paid time off hours from work.

I see the next decade as a time when my son will marry some woman my wife will hate, a daughter who will find pleasure in her work and not a family until it's too late, a wife who will sag with age.

And for me? A continuing battle with the waistline, the hairline, the lines in my face that seem to arrive overnight, and then fade throughout the day, or really it's just my eyesight .

And so if the end should come I won't fight it. I'm not one of those who wants to live to 120 and will fly to Denmark for some experimental treatment so I can stretch a six-month life sentence into seven months or ten or a year.

I only worry about the pain.

"Will it hurt?" is the first question I ask every doctor or dentist about every procedure and prodding. I hate physical pain because I can't run from it. Emotional pain is avoidable.

"I have been close to death," I told my therapist. "Not that I've almost died, but I feel close to it. Thinking of it, trying to grasp it."

"You have been acquainted with the night?" my therapist asked.

"Ennui" I told him half way through my four hundred and fifty dollar hour.

"Ennui?" he said in a tone that made it sound like a question.

"Boredom," I said this time, expecting him to know everything from Freud to Strunk and White. "That is my affliction."

"I know what it means," he said.

"You didn't seem to," I told him, still annoyed that we started the session three minutes late. Sometimes that married, or soon-to-be not married couple, that has the time before me goes over their allotted fifty minutes and knocks me back a few. But I never go over. I leave on time either because I start to gather my things with a couple minutes to go, or because he abruptly says, "See you next week," whether I'm in the middle of a sentence or a break in thought.

He thinks my problems aren't as severe as the married couple before me or the sad sack guy after me. The guy who lost his wife, I think. I don't know why I think that, but he looks lonely, doesn't wear a wedding ring, but dresses nice, like a lawyer about to see clients.

Since my problems aren't money or health, I'm not going broke or dying, it seems less dramatic or serious to him? There's nothing he's doing to make me feel this way, he would say, but I get this sense by the way he sometimes looks out the window like he's thinking, but he's just bored. Or the way he lets the couple ooze into my time. I shouldn't feel like I have to entertain him.

"There is a distinct lack of newness in this life of mine," I told him, "in case you hadn't heard."

"You've mentioned it," he said in his usual drone. "More and more since Nathan left for school."

Sometimes during therapy when I find that I have spoken about the same topic for too long I tend to make a change. Not because I am over it or I'm getting better or solved it in some way where he can take credit, but just the boredom of it. Or maybe I get embarrassed about the continuing spiral of emotions built on my sinking ship of privilege and ease.

That's really not how I feel my life to be, but that's what he is thinking, doctor know-it-all, doctor judgment, doctor sit there and let me answer my own questions.

I know that from his chair, behind his baggy shirt and ill-fitting pants, horrible instant coffee and a belly full of breakfast bars he is judging me and writing in his journal or telling himself that I am a spoiled middle age man with typical middle age man problems and he could be helping some suicidal kid or grieving widow if it wasn't for my time slot, but the truth is not many people would pay his price. So he needs me.

I can't stand his judgment, though he tells me it is getting in the way of my therapy, hindering my chance at success. But really, what is success?

Later that night the taillights come at me like red tasers, boring holes in my eyes. The rain is pouring as my car farts along through Washington traffic. These people can't drive in the rain. In Washington, the level of bad driving is one notch above, or below, the rest of the world. Here they drive in the rain as if it were snow, they drive in the snow as if it were ice and in the sun as if it's raining. They drive slower depending on the level of precipitation, but it starts a level behind every other civilized country.

"I've got the list," my wife says, trying to make things light as we inch along. "I just need you to verify and clarify." Her words come out all sing song-y. Even if they hadn't rhymed she would have powdered it with cheerfulness.

She knew I was tense. Even after 24 years of marriage I am no good at hiding it, my frustration with life comes at her in bursts of quiet.

"I can't do it while I'm driving," I said, the tension of the quiet, now finding its voice.

"It's your birthday," she said.

"It's your party," I said.

"You can't seem to find the time when you are home, or after dinner, or before bed, or during breakfast or after your Sunday run, or."

"I'll do it tonight," I said before turning up the sound of a Howard Stern interview on the radio.

The evening had passed as so many others do. I left the office around 5:30 and drove home in traffic and then to another dinner with another couple who are also recently empty nested and we had a piece of fish and a glass of wine. I got the house wine because I don't really know much or care much about the wine. And I spent the hundred and twenty five dollars and I tipped the valet and we drove home in the traffic and the rain.

It was ten o'clock when I got into bed, the baseball game was still bursting from the television when she came upstairs. My eyes were closed in faux sleep.

"I know you're not asleep," she said.

The diagnosis came the next day.

Something had chafed at me as I lay in bed a week earlier, my hand fishing in my pants for the rough patch.

"What are you doing?" my wife asked, never a fan of me with a hand in my pocket, let alone my underwear.

"Something hurts," I told her.

Telling your wife of twenty plus years that something hurts is akin to asking her if she let the dogs out. It gets a perfunctory response with the impact of a fallen paperclip.

She did not tell me to see a doctor and I did not tell her I would. And she did not ask again.

But as I searched for this rash or ingrown hair in a place where I would not be comfortable calling a doctor, I did feel what seemed like a third ball and at first I laughed, but it was too tender.

Now Dr. Ira Katz was telling me it was cancer.

He asked questions in an accusatory manner, of which I was not a fan.

"How long has it been there? When did you first feel it?"

But I heard him asking, "Why didn't you feel it sooner?" "Why did you take so long to come in?"

And then he told me it had spread, in a way to suggest it was my fault.

He quickly added it was curable, if they attack it now.

I also didn't like the military references he and the others kept using, we're not waging war on my nut sack.

The doctor couldn't stop telling me how lucky I was, even though my face was still warm from hearing the words cancer, at least as it related to me.

"The good options," he kept saying as he discussed removing my testicles, shooting me with radiation and medication that will make me "feel dreadful" for a while.

"But on the other side of this you'll feel like your old self," he said. Which didn't seem like such a great option to me.

"But without my balls," I said.

"There is hormone therapy, we've made great progress."

"Do you have both your balls?" I asked.

"I do," he said.

"Do you know what it feels like to not have both balls," I continued until he cut me off.

"Look, if I were a gynecologist I could still help you get through childbirth even thought I wouldn't know what it's like to push out a baby," he said. "Just like I can't relate to the experience of the hundreds of men I've treated over the past twenty years."

I couldn't argue with him and frankly didn't want to. And then I hit him with it. The money question:

"What if I do nothing?" I asked.

"That's not an option," he said.

"I think the choices are still mine," I said back. "My body, my choice?"

"What do you mean?" he asked, cocking his head like a dog hearing a far off can opener.

"Just what I said. What if I choose no course of action?"

"Then you will die," he said.

"Bad phrasing," I said, "because by the way, we're all gonna die, you may want to add that to your repertoire."

"It will grow," he began slowly, "although I don't know how fast really. I mean, we could test it. But most people come as soon as they feel it, and then it's usually still contained. But yours is not and so it will move faster and you will get sicker, and it will grow and you will get more uncomfortable. And as it metastasizes you will get into real trouble because it will affect multiple organs, multiple treatments all kinds of problems and complications."

"And pain?" I asked, the real question behind my questions. "How much will this hurt?"

"Pain?"

"Will I be in pain if I do nothing?"

"You came in because you were in pain," he said.

"I was uncomfortable," I said.

"It will start to hurt more," he said. "A lot more."

"Describe it."

"It all depends, but there is the procedure, which isn't pleasant and then the recovery and then the meds will cause minor problems, nausea, some muscle aches. Hair loss is not unlikely."

I took the literature and scheduled my follow up appointment.

That night we sat with another couple at another hundred and fifty dollar fish and wine dinner.

"Is it under-cooked?" my wife asked, pointing her fork at my half-eaten piece of black cod.

"It's fine," I said, but I wasn't hungry. Not because of the diagnosis or the fear of cancer, but my stomach just hurt, as if I'd swallowed a marble and it was trying to pass through my colon. I thought it was mostly in my head, you know you're told something is broken and it starts to hurt more.

When I spoke up midway through dinner my wife looked at me with the surprise of a spouse whose husband just woke from a twenty-year slumber.

The drive home was another replay or another post-dinner analysis, but I found it bothered me less. I always hated these discussions, the analysis of the other couple, what they are doing with their boring lives, the exchange of Risotto recipes, their spoiled kids and the great jobs they are getting, or the horrible people they are dating. But tonight it was tolerable. Maybe because I knew this discussion would not go on forever, because my forever just got shorter. Even as my stomach gurgled, there was calmness to it as the blabbing became more palatable knowing it would end soon.

Most mornings in the shower I would play with the new growth I would find, sort of like that scab you can't stop picking, or that piece of dandruff you might feel in your hair where you need to keep scratching. I would feel it when I put on my underwear and pants, or when I went to the bathroom during the day. But then it would settle into the back of my mind.

The morning was bright with the sun pouring through my windshield. I fumbled for the sunglasses for the first time in what seemed like weeks. A large swath of dust lay across both lenses that I rubbed out on my arm.

Sometimes the warm days would bring me down because they taunt me to go outside and make use of the rare sunshine in February. But now it was welcoming and I looked forward to a weekend hike and some work for a potential client.

The doctor's office left a message telling me I'd missed my appointment and asking me to call back to reschedule.

I erased it immediately and pretended like it never came.

"What's wrong with you this time," my wife said as I came in from the back yard with the dogs.

"What do you mean, this time?"

30

"You're limping," she said.

But she got distracted when the phone rang.

Weeks passed and I began to wonder, what is the doctor's obligation? He knows I have cancer, he knows I will die sooner rather than later if not treated, yet his office stopped calling after only 3 tries? Is that all I'm worth? I know they can't force me to come in, but still, shouldn't they be trying a little harder?

I soon became an expert on my body and its functions and fluids. Every ache that seemed odd or new, every bowel movement that hurt, the way food tasted, the sounds my stomach made as I lay in bed with Terry sleeping next to me.

I enjoyed having this secret all to myself. At dinner when friends asked how I stayed in shape it was the first time I realized my pants weren't fitting. I had stopped working out and felt less healthy, but something inside of me was eating away at the fat or the muscle, I didn't know which, but I was losing weight. Not in huge drops, I only weighed 175 at my peak, but little by little the pants grew on me, the collar on my shirt hung open, not quite another belt loop, but it was moving in that direction.

"How does it feel?"

I was surprised by the question as I ran my fingers over my stomach, thinking I felt another protrusion, like the one I saw in the bathroom earlier that day.

I must have looked surprised because Rick, our company attorney, asked the question again.

"This was the longest negotiation I ever remember you sitting through," he said. "You showed more patience than I have ever seen."

I didn't ever recall feeling this good about a deal, or more successful. We had worked long hours to get this signed. And while

31

the fruits of this work, the real money, wouldn't start coming for years, I felt a sense of accomplishment. Years three and four of this deal were years I would not see, although I really didn't know how long it would take for this cancer to kill me, but I assumed it would be sooner than that.

The following month a reminder for my next dentist appointment arrived on my desk. I looked at the date, two weeks in the future. I would of course be around for it, but did I want to go? I didn't expect to be around for my next one, six months later, so why go to this one? I remember the sign in the office from when I was a kid: "You don't have to brush all of your teeth, only the ones you want to keep." The goal is to keep your teeth your whole life, well put a check mark by it, there's no need to go beyond that.

The invitations for my fiftieth birthday went out. I'd never reviewed the invite list, Terry just got sick of waiting and decided the date would come and go whether I spent the time reviewing the people I liked or didn't like, the names of those we no longer spent time with and the people who were more obligation than preference.

Planning a party outdoors seems to be something you do if you were naturally lucky or stupid. But Terry always planned things outside and it was always the sunniest day of the year.

"But this is my birthday," I protested, "not yours. Maybe God will realize it's for me and make it rain."

Terry answered with some long slightly humorous answer that I mostly missed because for the first time I'd invoked God, a person who rarely had a seat at our table and I wondered.

Feeling closer to death or the end or the whatever, my focus on what it might be like would hit me at odd times, when people said things invoking religion or heaven and hell or even the word die, like "I almost died" after seeing a scary movie or being embarrassed in a public setting. The words would set me off on a course of thought that sometimes turned gory, like thinking about bugs in my casket and what if I wasn't really dead and I had to get out and I couldn't, like that girl I once read about. And then I would go over every indiscretion from the past 50 years and wonder if it really mattered, if someone else saw what I did and would then put me in judgment for it.

I found myself sitting in our children's bedrooms, stuck in time, old posters on the wall of basketball players no longer in the league, ticket stubs from long-forgotten concerts, a presidential library to their achievements before they left our house.

A "Grrrrr" sound coming from the corner of my son's room startled me. I reached over behind his desk to find a small plastic spaceman that hadn't been touched in probably ten years. Maybe longer? What do we do with all this discarded stuff? What do we do with pictures, the toys or clothes of people after they lose their usefulness?

The toy roared again in my hands. I flipped it over to see an on/off switch protruding from the spaceman's butt. I moved it on then off and the arms moved slowly, just a touch, as if a long dead item had one final thing to say.

Maybe this is how we die.

I'd never thought too much about it, the whole body and soul, another life, another place, thing. Except maybe on those rare occasions when I found myself inside a place of worship, a holiday, a wedding when I was too bored to listen and the sounds of the place just made me wonder. For the most part I was too busy being annoyed with this life to worry about another one. But now these topics invade my head like uninvited relatives and they don't leave. They just sit there between my ears as I play with this dead, or dying, toy in my hands. I felt tired at that moment and thought maybe, like this toy, we just run out of gas. Maybe our batteries die and we end up on the floor or in a corner, our structure still there, but everything inside is all turned off. Our on/off switch still in the on position but nothing moves, inside it's all hollow and quiet.

Or maybe, after months or even years we move again, even slightly, just a smidge. The gears and switches of our mind and body connect up in a moment like some small big bang and we move or sit up or think or whine or bark or yell. Maybe we aren't awake, something akin to sleepwalking.

Death, which always looked to me like a trap door, a way to escape the troubles of today without having to explain, now brought some sense of not dread, but fear. What if it's scary, that moment, the days after? The physical pain of the coming months wasn't the problem it was afterward when I would really be alone, even more than I am now.

The following week it is 19 year-old son who is playing with the dead toy.

"What do you think he would have done?" Jamie asks his sister.

"Where did you find this?" she asks.

"It was on my desk."

The children had come home for my funeral. The call from their mother was agitated, though not screaming. Most likely she'd taken a sedative, they assumed.

"The police are here," Terry said to our son, the same words she used to open the discussion with our daughter.

She waited after saying the first sentence long enough for them to ask why.

"It was a bus," she continued.

The suspense was too much for them, each asking her, "What are you telling me?"

She finally got it out, telling them about the crash, how it ran a red light, pushing my car into oncoming traffic. They didn't know if I died from the initial impact or whether it was the second car or the third. It didn't matter. Their father was dead and this was that phone call that they didn't expect to hear for another 20 years.

"He didn't live very long after the crash," the police officer guaranteed her. "He was gone by the time we arrived."

And now a week later, the shock still reverberating around the house, the siblings, who admitted they hadn't spoken to me in the weeks leading up to the accident, were talking about the blue felt diary filled with my familiar left-handed script.

"Do you think mom knew?" she asked her brother.

"And didn't tell us?" he said. "It's possible. I don't know what kind of secret pact a husband and wife make after their kids go off to college, but this isn't something you hide."

"Why did they stay in this big house?" she asked.

"Had to be depressing," he said.

"Nothing has changed," she said. "Those are the same sheets on my bed from high school."

"Do you think they ever used these rooms?" he asked.

"Dad must have if his diary was sitting on your desk," she said.

"He could have moved in here, for all we know," he said. "Maybe after the kids go away you worry less about how it looks and more about what you want. It's great, you can sleep in a different

35

bed, stay in a different part of the house if you want privacy. Have your own bathroom?"

"I never thought about it before," she said.

"About what?"

"About them," she said. "You know, their lives."

"She didn't know he was dying," my son said.

"Do you believe her?"

"Why would she lie?"

"Maybe she knew and didn't want us to worry," my daughter said. "Or maybe she is embarrassed he never told her."

"This can't be real," he said raising the blue book, the covers splayed open. "Maybe he was writing a story."

"A story," she said. "This was the world's most uncreative man and suddenly he's writing short stories about middle aged men who lie about having cancer."

"That wasn't what the story was about," Jamie said. "It's about a man who didn't want to live."

"It's about a man who kept secrets," she said.

"It's about a man who wanted something that was his own," he said, before tossing the book onto the vacant bed.

"Do we tell her?" the brother asked.

"She must have known," she said again.

"It was his secret to tell or to keep," he said.

"Then why did he write it down?" she said. "He wanted us to find out."

"But why?" he said.

"It's sort of a dicky move," she said. "Telling us, after he died, that he didn't love us enough to want to live."

"We weren't a part of this equation," he said.

"Then why did he write it all down?" she said.

"We weren't meant to know."

The doorbell, a familiar childhood sound, rang out, which set off a chain reaction of barking dogs and ringing phones.

They both left the room and prepared for another round of discussions with people from their childhood who would recount an anecdote about their dad and then say something completely innocuous like what a good guy he was.

But instead of a neighbor it was a white box with red postal stripes and an envelope.

It had been delivered, but the delivery person didn't wait for a signature or anything. The envelope had their father's name on it. Inside the blank business envelope was a typed letter with one line:

Office belongings: Peter Wolving.

They took off the top of the unsecured box to find a stack of books and folders, loose papers and a bound appointment calendar, the same type he had kept for years, unwilling to move to something electronic.

Their mother put her hand to her lips and went back into the kitchen. The brother and sister began fingering through the last of their father's belongings. The son flipped pages in his calendar, a voyeuristic thrill and fear.

He opened it to the final week of my life.

"Who is Doctor Katz?" he said.

"Never heard of him," his sister said. "Why?"

"Mom, who is Doctor Katz," he yelled. "Dad had an appointment today."

(Even though it was published this way, not sure I liked the ending. The other ending had a letter showing up saying is was not cancer....)

# Camping Alone, With Nick

*This is a story inspired by Deep Creek Lake in Western Maryland (where it was written) and of course, Northern Michigan. It was also just after the airing of the PBS documentary on Hemingway and so Nick Adams was definitely on my mind in April 2021. The story was quickly picked up by the* Umbrella Factory. *They did an impressive job of laying it out calling it the "New Face of Cool," although I don't know why. It's a dark piece but one that I really like because it reminds me of winter and snow and nighttime. I struggled with the ending for a long time, but thank goodness for deadlines to help you kick it out the door.*

YEARS AGO FRIENDS STOPPED ASKING RAY WHY HE WENT CAMPING alone in the winter.

It wasn't that they were satisfied with the answer. They never got one.

He'd just say: "Camping alone, with Nick."

It was deep into the icy season when Ray left his home in central Pennsylvania and drove three hours into the country to find the cabin at the end of the lane without directions. He'd grab the key from the windowsill, brush off the snow, and let himself in.

Even all these years later, he was unsure why the owner left the key out in plain sight. After all these years he wondered if there was any owner at all.

It was cold when he stepped inside. February cold. Crunchy snow beneath his boots cold. Too cold to take his jacket off. The lock hadn't frozen and since there was no running water, the pipes didn't burst. The only question was whether he could get the wood to light fast enough to generate some heat to make the night livable.

It was dark outside but the moon hung over the lake like a chandelier, lighting up the smoke that came from his mouth when he breathed.

He knew the routine, taking towels from his bag and laying them across the floor where he could sleep. In the morning he would get up with the sun and try to squeeze some water from the frozen lake's edge.

The trouble with the nights wasn't limited to the cold or the hard floor, but the fear of someone walking in and stepping on him or shooting him for trespassing.

But this night he made it through, and the cold was the worst of it.

Happy to see the end of darkness, he stood with the first rays of light and took the pot from the kitchen and slid through the back door. The house was shrouded in thick trees, which made him feel safe but also targeted, as if something hid beyond the broken brush. But it was only ghosts. He looked both ways before traversing the trail that led to the lake, crossing the spot where his friend's blood had soaked the earth.

Once at the water's edge, he dug his heel in where the grass met the ice, cracking the shallow spots until the water pooled. He sunk the bottom of the pot into the mud until it filled with frigid water, then hauled it back to the house, where he made orange juice from concentrate and coffee.

Once his body unstiffened, he took out one of the six peanut-butter sandwiches he'd packed and ate it along with the juice. What was left turned into coffee, which he kept on throughout the day.

He looked out over the quiet lake and dead trees and thought about the things he imagined were out there. The ones that howled at night, that scared him in his dreams. He thought of how he found the house on a trip years before. How he and Nick had hunted all day and stayed in their tent each night, talking about life in the country and why it suited them better than the suburbs where they found themselves the other 362 days out of the year.

Nick said he needed the quiet.

"These annual trips are the only quiet I get," he said.

"Then why do you talk so damn much?" Ray would counter.

"Because at home I can't get anyone to listen to a word."

"What makes you think I'm listening?" Ray said and they laughed.

The woods were silent except for their laughter.

Ray was married briefly but had no kids. "No harm, no foul," he'd say.

But Nick stuck with it. The first daughter came a few weeks after the wedding, and the next one arrived on their second anniversary. The girls were getting older and, as Nick put it, "more interesting," but he would never make enough money to make Maddy happy. At least that's what he told himself. Now he had a four- and six-year-old and refused to abandon ship, no matter how bad their lives made him feel.

Nick and Ray were best friends since they were playmates in kindergarten, locker partners in middle school, and a tag team on the high school wrestling squad.

They started what they called their camping trips when they were still in grade school. Nick's father would come home drunk, and Nick would sneak out the back window and wend his way through the neighborhood until he reached Ray's house. They'd lay out a blanket and try to listen to the quiet in between cars whizzing on the highway overpass. Soon they draped an old bedsheet through a couple of trees as a makeshift tent, telling Ray's mom it was their fort, but it was really just a hiding place. A forerunner to their trips.

Once they were old enough, they decided to head out to the woods in February because it was the week between their birthdays.

Even with the frigid temperatures, they insisted on sleeping in a tent so they would keep the tradition alive, discussing how they would only move indoors one day if the kids wanted to join.

The cold was the defining feature, which led to three rules: Move as much as possible in the daylight, keep your clothes dry, and light the fire before you need it. During one of the first years, Ray twisted his ankle stepping in a snow-covered hole. Nick carried him for a mile or so, and they always said Ray had the worst of it; at least Nick was still generating heat.

They kept moving, hiking, climbing, shooting things. They shot at anything that passed their way. The occasional bird or rabbit, it didn't matter. They were so far out that there were no rules or hunting season. They shot at tree limbs and birds' nests and any object with some distance.

They hiked all day, ate peanut-butter sandwiches, and drank either beer or whisky, depending on the hour.

The solitude and the distance from city lights brought out the stars and reminded them of the first time they saw those designs in the sky that became so familiar to them. As children they wondered what adulthood would be like.

"Your wife is gonna be so mean," Ray would say.

"Your wife is gonna be so ugly," Nick would say.

It was on their final trip together, when they were barely thirty years old, that Ray found the house he now slept in. He was struck dumb when he first saw it, wondering how, after all the years of walking these woods, he never saw it.

It was as if the place rose from the ground just when he needed it. It was the tenth year of their trip, and their guns were jamming from the frigid air. Nick banged his on a large rock rising from the frozen ground. Ray took a snow-covered stick to clean out the barrel.

Ray looked away every time Nick smacked the gun butt against the rock until he heard something that caused the birds to scatter.

Ray felt a tug at his back, but it wasn't his friend's hand but rather bits of shattered skull from the accidental gunshot that sprayed his jacket and knit cap in red and pink.

Ray didn't scream, instead just repeating, "Oh my God, oh my God," as he tried to figure out what to do, his friend's body already lifeless by the time he turned back. A river of red poured from a gaping head wound. Ray knew there was little he could do to save his friend. His first instinct was to stuff everything back in. Instead he ran. He ran up a hill, away from the lake, and it was then that the house appeared for the first time.

This was a great miracle to him. And he believed it would be the thing that would save him from this moment. A moment he wanted to undo with an urge stronger than anything he'd ever felt.

When he reached the house, he knocked, then pounded on the back windows, but nothing. He ran around to the front door to continue his pounding but there was no response. The house was as lifeless as Nick. He yanked at the door, shaking the knob. He looked in the side window, ready to punch through it, when he saw the key on the ledge.

First the house appeared and now a key. Things were lining up, presenting themselves before him; he was going to save himself from this moment. Maybe there was a doctor in the house or a first-aid kit or a magic wand, something to make it all better, to save his best friend, to save the father of those daughters.

He flung the door open violently, sticking it firmly into the drywall.

"Hello," he screamed, "hello, hello." But the house was silent and empty, save for his heavy breathing. He ran into each room, one dustier and quieter than the next.

There would be no final miracle. Just a cold, empty house. Finding it and the key were as unlucky as the gun going off in the middle of nothing. These fits of "luck" gave him hope. And in the time it took him to find the house and the key and arrive inside to the dread that waited for him, Nick's body had turned cold and blue in the moonlight.

That was the first night he slept in the house that was not his. The phone had been turned off and there was no gas, but it was indoors and the fireplace lit up.

Before inspecting the house further, he went back to retrieve Nick's body. He wanted to sling it over his shoulder and carry him, but he knew the gash in his head would empty and it was too awful. And so he reached under Nick's arms and pulled his best friend the fifty yards up the hill, creating two parallel paths in the snow.

Ray didn't sleep that first night either. His worry about the owners coming home was fourth on his list. First he worried about his friend's body, which he set in a screened-in porch on the side of the house. Second was how he was going to find the car and deliver the body back home. Third was how he was going to tell Maddy and the girls about what happened. It was just an accident. They must know that.

The next morning he hiked back to the car and returned to the house, where he laid his frozen friend in the back seat and then drove to the nearest hospital, where he explained what happened. He told them all the reasons why it could have happened and why he was unable to bring the body in the previous night.

They did all the paperwork, even called Maddy and told her what happened. They said his friend was in shock and couldn't talk.

In the ensuing months Ray lived a solitary existence, but it was what he wanted. He didn't need to talk it through or see friends. His friend was dead. Within a year Maddy and the girls moved back to her parents' in Maryland, and he never heard from them again.

The only sign of Nick that remained was the trip Ray continued to take. He'd gone back and found the cabin the following year. The key frozen on the ledge where he'd left it. When he returned nothing had moved—not the phone he threw to the ground when he tried it, not the blanket he'd slept on in the middle of the floor, not the matches he'd spilled, not the ashes in the fireplace.

And so the ritual began.

A silent weekend where he spent the nights on the floor of the abandoned cabin, hunting and hiking by day but violating the first rule of their friendship: No camping indoors.

Work was never consistent for Ray and only got lumpier once Nick died. Through the years of tumult, when jobs and money were scarce and human connection rare, he'd make the pilgrimage to the cabin.

He was still at it well into his fifties, even cheating a bit by bringing a small lamp and extra firewood. The cold was getting too much for him. He'd read by the fire and eat the sandwiches. He'd always bring enough as if Nick were still there. Sometimes he'd talk to the bread.

But one loop that continued to cycle through his head was the story. How it had happened. What to tell the girls or Maddy if he ever saw them again. In all the years they never called, never asked, never wondered anything more about his final day.

Then, one morning, a car pulled in as he was boiling water over the fire. He was in a pajama top and bottom with long underwear and a knit cap on his head.

He looked out the window when a man and woman in their late twenties stared at Ray's car as they walked to the front door, a different key already in hand. He grabbed his blanket and sleeping bag and backed up toward the fireplace, where he sat when they crossed the threshold to the house.

"Who the hell are you?" the woman asked.

"I'm sorry," he said.

"Why are you in our house?" she asked.

"I don't know," he said. "I didn't know it was yours."

"Well, did you think it was yours?" the man asked.

"I'm leaving," he said. "I'll just leave."

"You've made a mess," she said.

The mess had been accumulating for twenty-five years.

Ray looked around the room. There were books and bags he'd left over time, a set of cups, and a plate, a fork, a knife, and a spoon in a sealed plastic bag.

All the years passed through him as he looked around the small cottage. He remembered everything, going back to the day he saw it rise from the snow. The moment of horror when he realized the cottage was not a godsend.

"It's all coming down anyways," the man said to the woman.

"How long have you owned it?" Ray asked, knowing he'd been coming there since they were in diapers.

"About a day," he said.

"What's it matter to you?" she said.

Ray hadn't worried about someone walking in on him for many years. Over time bears and vagrants scared him more.

When his arms were full of belongings, he hurried out into the morning cold, shuffling along to his car, the door slamming behind him.

He pulled away from the house quickly as another car, with another young couple, sped past him.

The cars had Maryland license plates.

He knew he'd been lucky over the years, and even today, that the owner didn't have a gun or decide that calling the police was the best solution.

Driving away from the lake, Ray always felt the weight of his friend's loss. He usually left early in the morning, around the time he'd brought Nick to the hospital. And when he'd pass the sign for the hospital, something made him want to drive in and see if it was all a dream or whether it was the same—the same people, the same memory of where he parked, and how a stretcher carried his frozen friend inside.

But in all the years he just stepped on the gas and got home, except now. Maybe he knew it would be his last chance.

He pulled off and followed the signs to the county hospital. And it was all the same. Same time of year, same time of day. He parked his car and walked in through the sliding glass doors.

"Can I help you?" a woman sitting, in a nurse's uniform, behind a glass partition asked.

"I was here twenty-five years ago," he said. "I brought in my frozen friend."

"Frozen man," she said before he could finish.

"What?"

"Oh, nothing," she said.

"Yes," he said. "Were you here back then?"

"Seriously, that was you?" she said. "We just got a call on it last year."

"What do you mean?" Ray asked.

"A couple of women were trying to find out where their dad died," she said.

"But he didn't die here," he said.

"No, there was an address of a nearby cottage," she said.

And now the memories came back through the haze of a moment he tried to forget. He remembered how he had to show the police the place of the incident. He needed to prove his innocence with Nick's gun. The bloody snow scene.

So there was a record somewhere of the cottage. An address he never committed to memory. He could always just find the place by feel. A left at the lodge, a right around the lake, the clump of birches, the faded rhododendrons, the split tree. And while there was no paved driveway, he carved a path from all the years of driving in the mud right up to the front door.

He walked out of the hospital and thought about going back to the cottage to see the girls. He wanted to tell them how their father died. He wanted to explain what Nick was like, what they talked about, the meaning of these trips. But he knew it didn't matter. It was his need, not theirs. They had their memories, and he had his. So he turned onto the highway and accelerated taking one final look at the lake in the rearview mirror.

# Girl On The Balcony

*This story was composed as a journal entry as I sat in a hotel room in New Orleans in November 2018. I didn't look at it again for a couple of years, but since it was the first entry in the journal it popped up whenever I opened it. I had a deadline approaching and so I started nibbling at the idea that the women I saw from across the way jumped. Or did she?* El Portal *and* The Blue Lake Review *scooped it up.*

I WATCHED HER DIE.

Even from my hotel balcony five blocks away, I could tell. Even as the fading sun of the day dipped, its sharp angle blinding me as it hit off the casino's mirrored facade. I saw her put a leg over the rail and then the other and then she was gone.

I couldn't do anything from my perch or in my condition.

Even if she did jump, it wasn't much of a jump, more like a step over the edge, and then I heard people yelling.

I did get up from my chair, squinting to get a better view. But I soon sat down and was back at my newspaper. What could I do but wonder why?

During business trips like this, I don't get to the newspaper until late in the day. The nights are long and the mornings slow.

I asked the guys at the hotel whether they had heard about the jumper.

"Did you see her jump?" one of them asked.

"No."

"Did you hear her fall?" another said. "It's a horrible sound."

"How many bodies have you seen fall?" someone asked my interrogator.

"Well, none," he admitted.

"Great story, you saw nothing and heard nothing," another said.

"It's not up for debate," I told these drunk idiots. "It's like going to bed with a clean driveway and waking up with a snow-covered lawn. I can assume it snowed, even though I didn't see the flakes coming down."

"I didn't see nothing on the news," Gretna chimed in from behind the bar. "Maybe they waitin' on tellin' the family."

"Why did she do it?" Bobby, the most sentimental of the men at the bar that night, asked. "I mean how bad was it?"

It's impossible to know what's in somebody's head, of course, but I told them when I saw her standing just beyond the railing, I could tell by the angle of her face that she was going over.

"What the hell does that mean?"

"She paused," I said, "and just looked down, resigned to her fate. As if she had no choice. It was like somebody was sticking a gun in her back. But there wasn't anybody there, nobody giving her a push. Just the demons in her head that must have followed her around every day of her life."

"And I suppose you saw those demons from your balcony?"

"No, but they're there," I fought back.

It was after two in the morning, and the bar was closing by the time we began fighting about this. There will be time to fight about it again, or something else, the following night.

I couldn't stop thinking about the girl when I got back up to my room after another night in another hotel bar with these men I've

51

know for fifty years. Guys I grew up with and who I see when I come back to town three times a year. I say I'm here for business, but I just miss the bar. Drinking alone at home is hard.

I couldn't tell them this, but I *could* see her demons; they were all over her. And some of them were mine. I know they were there. An old drunk once told me about his demons. And I recognized them too. Like the ones I tried to outrun by leaving town. But they followed me to all those jobs in all those towns and into all those bars. They crash into my head without knocking. The ones who spend their time flying around my thoughts.

"You can't deny them," he said. "Not with drink, not with nothing."

But then he told me how to just live with them: "Since they are gonna be there, you might as well make friends with them," he said. "Bring out some tea and enjoy their company."

I told him I'd bring out the gin.

But not everybody can. Not everybody has tea or can afford gin. Not everybody can afford the advice of a man in a bar at 3 a.m. And so the demons float around our heads, and we don't know that we can do something with them other than be tormented by them. We don't realize there is another way. And finally, after so much time, the demons dominate our heads and we wind up dead.

We no longer recognize ourselves. We look in the mirror and see only demons, and that's what happened to the poor girl on the roof.

At night, when she turned off the lights or looked up to the stars or her dark ceiling, and all she saw were demons looking back at her.

"Did a girl die here last night?" I ask a short, balding man at the front desk of the building where I think it happened. Earlier in the day I stood, bloody-eyed, on my balcony with my toast and jam and counted the buildings and the streets.

The clerk looked around and nodded to a group of young people in their twenties, crying and consoling each other in the corner.

"I saw her," I told him before settling into the quiet so we could hear the chatter of the others.

"Why didn't you do anything?" one of the twenty-something men/boys asked another one.

"What did you say to her?" one of the girls/women said to one of the men.

"I wanted to help," another said.

"You were the last to see her," another said.

I was the last to see her, I thought.

"I wanted to see how I could help," I told the front desk man. But I knew there was nothing to do.

"Maybe you could have helped yesterday," he said.

I retreated to a café just off the lobby behind the front desk and sat with a coffee I didn't want.

Why did she do it? How bad was it? They all kept asking each other as if they didn't know her.

No one ever taught her how to deal with the demons, how to talk to them, how to distinguish between what the demons say and what they are telling you. These demons speak a different language.

The young group continued chatting and laying blame. They talked about someone and something about a fight. They asked why he couldn't have waited to break up with her. "You knew she was vulnerable."

When it got quiet I left my coffee cold, with more questions than answers, and sidled back up to the front desk clerk.

53

"Who's that?" I asked, nodding toward two sets of crying adults.

"Her parents," he said.

In one love seat was a middle-aged couple holding each other. The man's head was shiny and bald; the woman, more hair but a slightly more up-to-date outfit. In the other chair a man with salt-and-pepper hair and a woman about the same age. The inside positions were occupied by people who I later learned were the parents. Each engaged with their new spouse, their knees touching the person with whom they had made a child.

"Always about the food, you had to talk about food," the man said.

"She wanted to talk about it," the wife said, wiping her nose. "But she struggled, she just struggled."

They think it was their fault? They think it was the other one's fault.

"Humans are built to see the future," the front desk man said when the lobby cleared.

"What?" I asked, startled by this sudden utterance. Until then it was mostly nods and grunts.

"We are built to see the future and fear it," he went on. "There was a time when if we didn't learn how to see the future, we wouldn't recognize the danger, and we'd be eaten by dinosaurs. Slaughtered by the thing we would have recognized had we learned the language, recognized the signs, separated the animals from the plants."

There was a picture of a woman tacked up in the lobby. It was the woman. The jumper. The daughter. The friend. Seeing her up close now for the first time, she looked like my cousin Molly. My cousin was so pretty when we were growing up. Only a few years older than I, I had a mad crush on her. In the way that one could as the younger one but with the recognition that it would never lead to anything, never be returned because, in her eyes, I was just a punk. There was safety in that.

When you are kids, younger is younger; it's a subgrouping, it's the kids' table, it's like being in a separate fishbowl. You can't get there from here.

But that was before life made her face puffy, her stomach bulge, and her back hunch. Her first husband caused the lines because he was mean when he drank, which was a lot. And her second husband caused the bulge because he was just mean all the time. And the kids. Oh, the kids, they caused the hunch as they carried them through life. She tried to reverse it with the meds, and then the shots and the Botox and the makeup.

Age pulled her eyes down, and the shots pushed them up.

Age sucked her cheeks in, and the medicine puffed them back out.

Until finally her face was an unrecognizable yin and yang.

And so this woman whose picture now hangs on the lobby wall reminded me of Molly before the fall. This girl's face was pretty. It would never be deformed by age. And for that fleeting moment, when I watched her from afar, I wondered how she got there. Logistically.

Usually the rooftop of an apartment building is hard to get to, except in movies.

Turns out she didn't live there, which makes her escape to the roof even more improbable, impressive. I heard one of the earlier lobby gatherings talking, and their theory was that she was a guest at a party, and she wandered up there looking for the bathroom.

But the guy at the front desk shook his head. He'd heard there was shouting. She was embarrassed or someone broke up with her, and she'd had enough and decided she needed some air, and then, once up there, she took the opportunity.

"She regretted it," he said.

"How do you know?"

"Suicide survivors, you know, the ones who try but don't die. Almost one hundred percent of them say as soon as they step off the bridge, they regret it. Falling through the air, they all wished it were a bungee cord that would pull them back up."

But was this woman being chased by her demons or was it more opportunistic?

Like getting divorced. Everybody thinks about it at some point. As one longtime couple said, "We both wanted a divorce but, thankfully, never at the same time."

Never that moment where opportunity meets the moment. Maybe she never wanted to kill herself, but after a bad night, had the opportunity opened up?

As the sun sank into Lake Pontchartrain, she found herself on that rooftop with this demon on her shoulder, or the boy who broke up with her, or the father who picked on her, or the friend who didn't stick up for her. It wasn't one thing. It wasn't one of them now crying in the lobby. It was all of them. And so she took that small step over the rail and left it all behind.

She was silent as she turned her body, midair, from feet first to head first, as if she was completing a hands-free dive into a warm infinity pool. But instead of waiting for the warm water to welcome her in, it was the cold, hard cement that crushed her skull and broke her neck, I imagine.

But there was no body.

People said they saw a body going down.

I saw a body stepping over the side.

My new front desk friend said he spoke to the papers, and there were others like me who said they saw a woman on the roof of the sixteen-story building.

But when the reporters dug deeper and asked if they saw her jump, no one could say for sure.

When they checked with the hospital, there was no patient with a crushed everything.

When witnesses were rounded up, they said, "She must have." And I said, she must have.

The sign over the picture in the lobby just said MISSING.

In the evenings I go down to the hotel bar to drink with my friends until I feel I am ready for sleep. Sometimes it takes longer than others. They say alcohol is the wrong way to do it, but I don't know of any other way to quiet the world in a way that lets me rest.

When I feel the demons have all flown away or at least had a drink with me, I go out on my balcony and watch the lights through the cigarette smoke, and I look for the girl they never found.

Each night I'm out there, I watch for her and hope maybe this time I can stop her. The pretty girl who climbed over the railing, the girl who did not jump but disappeared from her life and her family and her problems without ever having to endure the pain. I look for her on streets and in the bars; I long to see the face I never met. I want to teach her how to talk to demons, not just drown them out with gin or crush them from sixteen stories up.

I want to tell her it will be okay.

# Counting Heads

*The title was inspired by a story a friend told me and the phrase "counting heads" stuck with me. But when the story just wasn't coming together I asked my daughter Natalie and her friend Raffi, both swimmers and lifeguards, what to look for when a person is drowning. I had the Village Swim Club in mind, which is the one we went to in Southfield Michigan. No one drowned, that I remember, but I definitely scraped my leg along the side.* Borrowed Solace *published it in May 2021. A friend who read it said, "you have a dark side."*

BILLY WAS GONE BEFORE THE AMBULANCE LEFT.

Twenty-three, twenty-four, twenty-five.

Sally wasn't good at math.

Maybe if she were, or the sun was at a different angle, she'd have seen the girl or heard the noise.

Some said it was Billy. The boy. The friend. The boyfriend?

He was the distraction, trying to make her jealous.

Maybe it was the fight with her mother from earlier in the day. She wasn't going to be late to work, no matter what her mother said when she woke her.

"I set my alarm," Sally screamed, pounding her fist into the pillow, making space for her matted hair. But her mother continued, flicking the light switch on her bedroom wall on and off. The cigarette dangling from her mother's mouth illuminated in the darkness and then vanishing in the light.

"My bathing suit is fine," was the next thing they argued about, sensing her mother's disapproval as she walked down the stairs. "It doesn't show too much," she said to herself. "And why can't a lifeguard wear a two-piece?"

The sunscreen bunched in globs on her face, but she couldn't see it until the end of the day. She didn't want to burn, but she didn't want to clump either.

"Nobody looks at the lifeguard," her mother said. "The lifeguard best be lookin' at everybody else."

But she was looking for Billy. He said he would fill up her water bottle and it shouldn't take this long.

She was a lifeguard and how was she supposed to guard their lives from everything?

"I'm only one person," she told her mother after coming home from the interview. "Two eyes is all I've got. That's as high as I can count."

Count the heads, she was taught, and when you're finished counting, count again.

Twenty-three, twenty-four, twenty-five.

But the sun was in her eyes and Billy was somewhere out there.

The sun no longer felt good, as it did in the early morning before the haze burnt off. Now it was hot, baking on top of the already well-burnt shoulders of Sally Trimmen, who everybody called Sunny.

The blond hair, only whiter at this point in August. Every day by the pool, high up in the chair, even closer to the sun.

"I was hoping there was somebody to save so I could jump in the pool," she told her mom. "It never happens."

"That's the point, hon," her mom said.

She didn't come there to sit all day and get burnt. She was there for a job.

"You're there to impress the coach so he'll recommend you to that good college," her mother said.

"I don't do any swimming," she said. "I just sit there all day, how is that impressing him?"

But now the summer was almost over, and she was glad to see it end. There would be a week after the pool closed, before Billy went off to college. They needed to stay together. She had to keep him interested just until the end of the summer, and then she would show him everything and he would want to stay with her when he left in the fall. She imagined that on the weekends she would drive to college to see him. But first this was gonna be their time. Their special time, the most special.

Now she wished for colder temperatures. Her job of sitting all day was turning into a waste of time. Time she could spend with Billy. Or, if her mom really wanted her to get into those colleges, she could have spent the summer training and getting her times down, but instead she sat all day.

"Lifeguards aren't guarding anything," she screamed at her mother one night when she had to stay home.

"You have work in the morning," her mother said.

"You have work too," Sally shot back. "Maybe you should stay in tonight!"

But then Billy told her how good she looked up there, and then she liked it. At least when he was there.

So she stayed. Only two more weeks.

Twenty-three, twenty-four, twenty-five.

She kept counting heads, but there were too many kids crowding on the diving board.

It didn't count as a save, but earlier in the summer, a small boy, maybe six or seven, didn't grab the silver handrail on the diving board and fell sideways onto the concrete. He cracked his head and she had to run over to help, but by then some adults were there, one was a doctor, and she had to keep watch on the pool, and blow the whistle three times so everyone knew.

The diving board was always where the trouble started, kids pushing in line (not her problem), kids falling off backward (not really her problem), kids on the board not waiting for the earlier divers to clear (her problem).

Where did that one kid go, the one with the pink head cap?

Her heart raced for a moment.

Maybe she got out.

So she started counting again.

She saw Billy near the snack bar eating a hot dog and a Coke. Where was her water bottle? The one he went to fill. He was talking to a girl. Who was that?

Only another hour and she would be off. And where was Megan? She was supposed to be there early to take over.

Twenty-three.

Is that girl flirting with Billy?

Twenty-four.

Is he flirting with her?

Twenty-three?

Why is it the hottest day of the year? She was sweating so much she couldn't even get the lotion on, it just mixed with the sweat and floated away into her eyes.

Sally was four years old when a coach first noticed what kind of swimmer she could be.

Flapping her legs in the shallow end, her mother holding her hands. There was something in the way she kicked, or maybe it was in the way her mother wore a bikini top when all the other moms were covered in layers of draperies.

A man in a small bathing suit and a whistle around his neck called over to them and asked if Sally was a "serious swimmer."

"She can be," her mother shouted above the noisy municipal pool crowd. "I mean, she's not even five yet."

When the man didn't react, she added: "I was quite a swimmer in high school. A natural, you might say."

By the time Sally turned seven, she was practicing three days a week. That escalated to five times a week, and soon there were swim teams, swim camps, medals, and ribbons, and until she moved away, people would ask: "Are you the swimmer?"

"Yes, I'm the swimmer," she would say.

She loved being "the swimmer" when she was in grade school.

In middle school, it made her a star and covered up for trouble with grades.

Chlorine became the smell of her success.

But by the time she started thinking about college, she was getting sick of it. And then the boys started noticing. And she could wear swimsuits and she got boobs and maybe swimming wasn't that bad. At least the moments before and after the meets. The bus rides to and from, the locker room, sitting on deck for all those hours as she pranced in her suits and newfound curves.

"She would be great," her mother told the head of the country club, when she was sixteen. They weren't members, never could be, but when her team had a swim meet, her mom would walk through the club as if she belonged. Maybe ask for a lemonade or club soda at the bar, and then spike it with something from her purse, giving herself a country club pour.

One night she was the equivalent of three cocktails deep when she told the head of the country club her daughter would be a perfect lifeguard. "She's very conscientious."

By the time her mom and the head of the club returned from somewhere out of sight, her lifeguarding career was launched. This dovetailed with her interest in Billy, who took tennis lessons across the parking lot.

But the summer was ending, and Billy was going to college, and she still had another year of high school, and everyone else was trying to beat their best times.

"It's less than a second," her mother kept saying. "You can knock it off if you don't eat dessert."

What did she know?

"Coach says we need to eat after practice," she said.

"Maybe you need something other than Twinkies," her mother said.

Who was Billy talking to?

Sally was thirsty and it was hot, and she couldn't reach her shoulders for more lotion. There was no one to help. Why was there never anyone to help her? A lifeguard can't guard against everything, can't guard against the sun *and* the water *and* the other girls *and* Billy *and* all those kids.

Twenty-three, twenty-four, twenty-five.

The lifeguard can't un-clump the lotion and make the sun go down and count the kids and make Billy like her. But that's what they were asking her to do.

It was still hot when the girl was taken away in the ambulance and the police asked her why she wasn't in the lifeguard chair. Sally was dabbing an overbleached towel on her bloody leg, which made it look worse than it felt.

Her leg bled because just before the accident, she stood up and gestured to Billy, shaking the bottle of sunscreen, but he didn't see her. So she climbed down to make her point, and to see why he was talking to that girl.

That's when she noticed Billy was talking to her mother.

That's when one of the kids screamed.

A drowning body doesn't float. They teach you that in lifeguard training. There's even a video when they show you how they sink to the bottom and people step on them.

She looked across the pool. What number was she on? She scanned the shallow end. What was happening? She got close to the edge, but nothing.

Twenty-five? Twenty-three?

The screaming came from the deep end, where there was already blood in the water. Lots of blood. The lifeguard chair was empty. Sally's legs hurt. Billy and her mother were looking at her. The screaming got louder. She dropped her bottle of lotion and leapt in.

She had been trained to jump from the chair, but now she was on the deck, and she scraped her leg along the side of the pool when she dove in. She grabbed the girl, who was still floating. Sally started crying. A siren came closer and closer.

Blood smeared along Sally's arms as if she'd painted it on with a thick brush. The blood from the girl's head mixed with the blood from Sally's scraped thigh and spread out across the pool like mist.

Sally held the girl's bleeding head on her chest as she swam to the pool's edge. Why was there so much blood? This wasn't in the film.

Two parents helped pull the girl safely onto a beach towel. Before Sally could administer any first aid, two men in twin blue outfits rushed in and pushed her aside.

Soon the summer ended and Billy left. Her counting was wrong, but it didn't matter. The girl had hit her head on the diving board. Sally didn't know how she didn't hear it. No colleges wanted her.

"My life is over," she screamed into her pillow.

"Your life? Your life? You have your whole life to fix this. What am I gonna do?" her mother yelled back, pacing Sally's bedroom floor, creating a path across the carpet. A path that lasted weeks until Sally vacuumed over it. Hoovering up the crumbs from the cookies that fell from her bed. A new nightly ritual where she ate the entire bag of Double Stufs because she was no longer interested in losing weight or time.

This was all before she graduated high school and moved one state over, where she got a job at a sub shop making overstuffed sandwiches for people who wouldn't recognize her name from the paper. It would be another fifteen years before she finished college at night, when she was in her thirties. It was before she adopted a daughter of her own.

Sally didn't die that day, and neither did the young girl.

But now, thirty years later, Sally was standing straight as plywood in her mother's bedroom.

Her daughter, just past her twelfth birthday, was sitting on the floor in a sea of ribbons, medals, and newspaper clippings.

"Are all these yours?" her daughter asked.

"Yep," Sally said.

"You were a swimmer?"

Sally sat on the floor with her daughter and, for the first time in decades, fondled the engraved medals and let the ribbons flow through her middle-aged hands. Hands now riddled with sunspots because she can't take the feel of sunscreen on her skin.

Sally doesn't know whatever happened to Billy. The swim club closed after the lawsuit. She'd only been back home a handful of times since the accident. The newspaper articles were unbearable, but her mother couldn't find a way to get out.

Sally felt the rise of nausea in her throat when she drove past the old swim club parking lot on the way to her mother's apartment. The swim club is now a retirement community.

Her daughter draped the heavier medals around her neck.

"Is this why you don't let me swim?" her daughter asked, pointing to the newspaper articles with harsh headlines, which were mixed in with the medals.

"Yep," she said.

"But you still swim," her daughter said. "Why can't I?"

"Don't you always tell me the pool made my hair smell funny?" Sally said.

"Yes," her daughter said, "but it washes out."

"Some things you can't wash out," Sally said.

"I like when you smell like a swimming pool sometimes," her daughter said.

"That's something I have to live with," Sally said.

"I want to smell like you," her daughter said.

"Not you, baby," Sally said. "You ain't never gonna have to smell like us."

# No Upside

*I kept this essay in because I reference it so much. To me it is the ultimate middle age story, and middle age choices seem to be my oeuvre. It was published in the* Avalon Literary Review *in the Fall of 2020 and I sent hard copies to many of the people involved in the actual episode. They enjoyed reliving the idiocy.*

"Why did you do it?"

"What do you mean?"

"The upside was minor. But the downside. Well, you saw the downside."

I thought I wouldn't make it up the stairs.

It had gotten hot.

The sun on my neck and the slight sweat sloshing down the collar of my recently purchased jersey.

I grabbed the railing. It was still cold from the pre-game.

I looked back at my son, his eyes fixed on the football field, so he wouldn't see what might happen next.

My feet kept moving, albeit slowly, up the stairs, one at a time, another, then another, each step heavier than the previous, as if my jeans were being soaked in water. I reached the top, wobbled a bit, and thought the lightheadedness and the fuzzy taste in my mouth could be cured by a cold Coke and some salty peanuts.

I made it to a guy standing behind a mountain of peanuts, and I squeezed out the words for a small bag and a drink. I must have given him money because he didn't chase after me as I walked away, looking for a bench or a place to rest and refill my system.

My eyes felt half closed, so I struggled, but couldnt get a clear line of vision to anything except a wall that I slid down; again the cold of the morning still in it kept me conscious.

I almost choked on the peanuts, there was minimal chewing, and whatever was stuck in my throat was washed away as I slurped on a double-wide straw. I washed my salty hands on the striped cup's condensation. But I continued to flag, my energies drained by something inside me, like I'd swallowed a great sponge and I was devoid of the liquid and nutrients that kept me afloat. My shoulders were unable to bear the weight of my arms. I needed help. I didn't want to end up here with no one, my fifteen-year-old son in the seats alone. I couldn't feel my cell phone.

I managed to rise from the stadium pillar, my vision worsening, until I saw a group of medics surrounding a stretcher that lay across the back of a four-wheel all-terrain vehicle. I don't know how many of them patrol the stadium throughout the game, but it was divine that they were parked there, paying me no heed. I dropped the soda and peanuts. As if in slow motion, they hit the ground and splashed over my shoes and jeans as I approached the four people. The sound or the splash must have shifted their attention because when I went down, I didn't hit the floor. They must have caught me.

A moment earlier I was another middle-aged man in a replica jersey who looked like any of the other 110,000 people there that October Saturday.

Maybe I took another stumble or two, but soon I was on the stretcher, a siren blared, and I went in and out of consciousness. My eyes opening and closing, the sun glaring down.

The gurney was cold and hard, each bump in the pavement painful as the sun sprayed my face.

At some point my eyes went fully closed, but I could hear the sounds and voices of the people in the crowd talking to one another, ignoring the sounds that had been so clear to me. The sounds that told a crowd to move, someone important is coming or something important is happening. The voices of a crowd always sound the same. There is something about the voices and languages blended together that makes the same sound no matter where you are. But in my state of semi-consciousness, it was like the perfect smoothie where nothing was recognizable: I couldn't tell the blueberries from the spinach, the peanut butter from the milk. I used to play a game with myself, trying to pick out the one voice, the one conversation, and follow that thread, but this afternoon it was all mashed.

Wait, is that a recognizable voice? A friend's wife chasing the vehicle as it honked and sped through the mass? Was she saying my name? No matter how loud the vortex of voices, our name leaps out. It blurred until I was in the shade of a tunnel and then in a bed, hooked up to an IV filling me with fluids.

I would soon learn that the underground MASH unit of a Big Ten fall football Saturday is made of primarily three kinds of people: the overdone undergraduate, the middle-age mistake, and the later-in-life slip.

The overwhelming majority are undergraduates who overdo it. They are propped up in beds by a pillow fort created by the medical staff, their head bowed; a large, red, plastic cone hangs upside down in front of their face, attached by a thin string around their neck. They look like sleeping birthday-goers, but actually they are just drunk students with a crudely derived puke-catcher around their neck. The only sounds coming from them are gags.

The next group are a much older set. Mostly men, north of seventy years old, who are at the games as long-ago alumni or grandparents. They have fallen and they can't get up. They are there for twisted ankles, crushed knees, and broken hips on the slippery floor or steep steps that allow 110,000 people to gather in one place. The sounds from them are the embarrassed whispers into their iPhones to their spouses about how they will get home, how they are feeling, and whether they can get in touch with doctor so-and-so, or their friend, or the generalist, or the son-in-law, the doctor.

I am in the smallest group. The middle-aged alum who come back to campus and make mistakes that hit us in the face so hard, we can't believe we asked for it.

There is embarrassment but there is also some legend that emanates from the mistake, the moment.

After two bags of fluids are pumped through my body, my son finds me with the help of some friends, and the lies flow to everyone in my family, my son as well as the wife and daughters who were home in another state. All are told various versions of how I got dehydrated on a hot day in a full stadium.

There is no discussion of the candy a friend handed me. Not so much a friend as a guy I once knew in this town, but at a time that seems so distant, it's as if it didn't happen to me. The memories so faded that it's like a movie I'd seen or book I'd read years before, and my recollection is now fond but not continuous. There are moments, not even vignettes, just moments that I can remember with great fondness in my belly but completely without detail.

So when this person I once knew asked me if I wanted a candy, which looked homemade in its ill-fitting wrapping, I didn't hesitate. I began licking it surreptitiously as we walked into the stadium. And the mistake I made is the one I laugh about when I see others do it. It's the one we warn our kids about, and if they made the mistake, it would be laughable as long as the consequences were benign.

Having done almost no drugs in the ensuing thirty years, I expected this one to hit me with some pop. But there was nothing. Like the girl in *A Chorus Line*, I felt nothing. So instead of letting the sticky mess fall to the stadium floor to dance with the dropped popcorn and hot dog wrapper, I held it tightly between my thumb and forefinger and continued licking until my son said he was hungry and I decided to stand up and shift the universe against me.

And after I have been wheeled out of the secret underground hospital with the other "patients," I am left on the sidewalk with my wheels locked until a friend and my son arrive with a car to take us back to the hotel. After I miss dinner and fall into a twelve-hour death sleep, I am walking to get a bagel, egg, and cheese sandwich the following morning with a fraternity brother whom I have known for twenty-five years.

Like most of these friends, we flow in and out of each other's lives; birthdays and anniversaries get phone calls. We show up for the big birthdays, the fortieths and fiftieths, something special for one of our kids, the death of a parent.

But on this day he is checking in to make sure I survived the night, to make sure my son and I get some food in our system before flying home. He is there to put me on the spot and ask me the question that I still can't answer. It struck me then and has for ensuing years as I seek answers about our aging lives.

"Why'd you do it?"

Just a few words, a question that didn't seem all that penetrating at the moment. I let it sit there as we crossed the street in the chilly morning air.

"I mean, what's the upside? Maybe the game is little more interesting?" he asked, tilting his head, trying to get my attention or at least eye contact.

"That's the whole upside, right? A little more interesting? But the downside? The downside is huge. The downside is, well, what happened. Your son alone in the stadium, unsure of where his father is. Friends looking for you. If David's wife hadn't seen you on the stretcher, I don't know how we would have found you."

"This is everything," I say, finally responding to his questions wrapped in questions.

We are in line at the bagel place, and I am feeling around my pocket for money, but all I feel is my hotel key card.

"Everything has a big downside now," I said. "All our mistakes. We have homes and mortgages and kids and spouses and credit card bills and debts and obligations. It isn't just that people rely on me; there are lots of people and things that I owe."

"That doesn't answer the question," my friend said. "I know there is downside. And I know you know the imbalance here. So why do you still do it? It's a bad bet."

"I didn't do it because it was a good bet. I did it because it was a bet I could make. That's all I wanted. Something new. Something I could try that I hadn't done in a while to make me feel different than this."

"Different than what?"

"Different than the everyday. All the bad things I don't have in my life. I'm well-fed, I have shelter and clothing and love."

My voice caught on love. Because that's the one thing you don't think about when you are counting your blessings. It's the one thing that isn't part of the equation. The equation you run through when you are making decisions that turn out poorly.

"I was here at my alma mater with my friends and my son, and it should have been enough. But it wasn't. I don't know why. But there is *nothing* left in life that has a big enough upside. Everything has a small upside. And everything with a small upside has a huge downside. And so every once in awhile, I need to do it. Otherwise."

"Otherwise what?" he said, his voice louder than it should be in this Sunday-morning restaurant.

"Otherwise I don't know," I said. "Otherwise I'll die."

"This is how we die," he said. "By making these mistakes. These judgements where the scales are so clearly tipped in the wrong direction."

"That's not how we die," I said. "It's by not taking those risks, those shots with the big downside."

"You take the big downside shots when it's something worth getting. You take the big shot going for the brass ring. You take the big shot when it's worth the potential downside."

Before I could reply he said, "And it's never worth the downside."

I didn't respond because I knew he was right.

But I also knew that there was no way to explain it, no way to really justify it because it was a bad decision. But if I'd gotten away with it, without incident, and then you asked me, would I do it again?

You bet I would.

And now that I've tumbled through the downside and I know how bad it can be—scarring my child, scaring myself, lying there helpless in a cave of illness, unsure of what was happening to my body as it careened toward the unknown—would I do it again?

I would.

# The Rise of the Parking Lot

*This essay was the starting point for other parking lot stories. I tried like mad to get it into a national daily, but no takers.*

THEY DIDN'T PAVE PARADISE AND PUT UP A PARKING LOT.

During Covid the parking lot became paradise.

It used to be a black top, concrete, yellow lines and parking blocks.

Now it's bingo halls, motels and movie theatres.

Of all the unexpected turns of this Pandemic the rise of the parking lot is another improbable one. The much-maligned asphalt desert that layers over the country's green spaces has become a haven of lost activities.

When everything closes, the parking lot opens up.

It began with Covid testing. Long lines in empty lots, swabbing people's brains until they cried uncle.

Red states and Blue agree that parking lots are the place to be:

- In Indiana one organization bragged about how popular its parking lot bingo became
- A religious organization in New Orleans performed it's rituals with "Shabbat on the lot"
- Drive-in movies light up the night in lots from the Michigan to Yankee Stadium.

75

- The expansion of farmers' markets in Maryland, "no-contact" play zones in North Carolina, protests have filled lots everywhere, and in Las Vegas the unhoused have found public shelter.

Not just social hotspots, they've become wifi hotspots as students gather outside schools, McDonalds and Starbucks searching for internet access.

For non-students, parking lots became digital lifelines with the closure of cafes and libraries.

"Virtual Marathons" became a thing as people ran alone around car-free mall lots.

One enterprising Minnesota mom got her friends to meet in the trunks of their minivans in an empty lot.

And family occasions have found new settings as engagements, surprise bridal showers, weddings, marriage certificate distributions and of course the big gender reveal parties have all moved to the lot.

Instead of being stop-over country, they've becoming destinations.

And there are reverberations as the demand for America's two billion parking spots is down 90% (for parking that is) a series of startups have jumped into the fray charging fees for the unused space. But so far Freedom is just another word for concrete.

The $700 billion concrete market is growing at a brisk pace and looking for a coronavirus bump.

Even politicians aren't immune to its appeal. Rep. Matt Gaetz quarantined himself in a Walmart parking lot after coming into contact with someone who tested positive for the virus.

Some stories have happy endings like the woman in Nashville who got hired by the Kroger grocery store. She been living in their lot.

Others not so much, like when Charlotte police were forced to break up a parking lot birthday party after concerns about a lack of social distancing.

Post-Covid we won't need to rebuild America, just pave over it.

# The Secret Lives of Parking Lots

*A variation on my parking lot period was this winning entry into the* Writers Digest Personal Essay Award *contest in October 2020.*

THERE ARE PEOPLE IN THOSE PARKED CARS.

I hadn't noticed.

The school near my home is closed due to Covid-19, yet most days the parking lot is full.

It's a religious school, artifacts hang from the walls and I wonder as I pass each morning, are the people in their cars here to pray?

I spy a tall man in jeans resting his steaming cup of coffee on the back of his flatbed, staring out at the empty soccer field looking as if he is secretly filming a Folgers coffee commercial.

Audible grunting a few cars down leads me to a woman, her car parked between two white lines, a yoga mat and weights fill up the other spot as she squats and stretches, pushes and pulls, oblivious to the dog walker scurrying by.

A man in a small convertible reads a newspaper while sucking on a cigarette.

A woman splays her legs around a canvas as she paints from the concrete.

Some days the lot is ablaze with quiet activity in hermetically sealed vehicles. Usually the cars are parked one space apart like men at a row of urinals. Other days they are askew as if they were stopping curb-side for a pizza,

In between these pods of people the dog-walkers meander, the bike-riders slalom, a man pulls two kids in a red plastic Radio Flyer, and parents grab their children as engines fire up.

As the quarantine lingers so do they.

They turn off their cars and open the windows, and their world opens up to me. Their voices bounce off the doors in the morning stillness, their stories become clearer as I hear one, then another and another.

"I can't talk long."

"I just had to get out."

"It's gonna be okay."

"I can't take much more of this."

"Why would he do this?"

There are practical reasons why they are here.

No longer just social hotspots, the parking lot is a Wi-Fi hotspot as students cling to the walls searching for internet access.

But for many it's something else entirely. It's not just a digital lifeline searching for a good signal.

Gabriel Garcia Marquez said: *"Everyone has three lives: a public life, a private life and a secret life."*

They are here for the secret life.

They are here for the relationship now relegated to phone calls, the conversations they hope vanishes into the ether, the release they cannot get in a house full of unattended kids. They are here to consume Triscuits with cheese whiz, Coke out of the bottle, ice cream from the carton, and small bottles of alcohol they usually get from the corner store near the office. They are here for the quiet.

All the things they did before the quarantine when the kids were at school, when they had a private office, when they had a commute.

Our public lives are filtered through Zoom.

Our private lives are confined within the walls of our homes.

But the secret lives are the ones that have been edited out by the quarantine.

There are still secrets, they are just housed in a parking lot or in the back seat of a car outside a vacant building.

They didn't pave paradise and put up a parking lot. During Covid the parking lot became paradise.

It has also become a soccer field, a bicycle track, a workout room, a coffee house, a diner, a back porch, a dog park, a phone booth, a bar, a rec room, an office park, a confessional, a synagogue, a hotel room, a movie theatre, a lunch counter, a drive-in. It's a place where people can work out the secrets of their life, where they can act like no one is watching.

# The Rabbi's Story

*I wrote this a few years ago but couldn't get it published. So I dug it out during Covid and re-worked it, sped up the action and changed the ending. The* Jewish Literary Journal *picked it and then* Fig Tree Books *published it. Even though it's based on a true story, I received a number of calls from friends after it was published asking for clarity. The protagonist is the real-life Rabbi who rented me a Torah for our kids' Bnai Mitzvot. He may still be in jail.*

THE TOWN WHERE MY GRANDFATHER WAS BORN IS DEAD.

It isn't just the name of the town that died, subsumed by a larger city, but the entire country is no more. The people fled before the war, and the ones who couldn't, or wouldn't, now lie in shallow graves all around the few kilometers that surround the city square.

It is a place so remote that there is no push to regenerate the Jewish people, to discover the grounds where the synagogue once stood. The people there don't remember a time when there was a Jewish community. They don't remember the names of the Jews who walked their streets.

Even so I find myself on a flight, to a flight, to a flight to try to get there to find something that I didn't know I was looking for. The names, faces, and bodies that once called this place home are now dust scattered to nearby towns and float along the waters that in the past one hundred years only took people away from here. It gets emptier each year. And finally one day it will be wind.

81

But now I am on way looking for a hint of what was.

The town was never alive for me, now three generations removed. The faces in the faded pictures always looked so sad, like they knew it was coming, the way you feel a storm that is still miles away.

I always imagined it was a sadder time. Everybody had a sibling who died or a sister who didn't make it through childbirth. Diseases wiped out families; fires weren't put out in time. They must have always hurt.

Until I found the Torah. Or rather, the Torah found me.

I never asked how the Rabbi who found the Torah, found me, but there must be a list of all of us, the descendants from this deserted hamlet. Descendants who had decided that even if it was a shitty little town, good people came from it and so it was worth remembering, from a distance.

And so every year there was a dinner honoring the people who had settled. I think a lot of them came for the jobs, the factories, the Midwest. The American towns that couldn't have been more different than where they came from, but they arrived nonetheless and became Americans.

Their children were real Americans, with American names like Bill and Johnny. But as these children aged, sometime in their 40's or 50's, they wondered anew about where they came from. In the morning when they looked in the mirror and noticed the cracks in the face, the lines along the eyes, this dispersed diaspora wondered where they fit in to the narrative.

That odyssey started for me when the Rabbi, who pitched himself as the "Torah Hunter," called to tell me I was in luck.

Instead of erasing the town by burning it down, the Nazis just killed the people and changed the names. So the synagogue became the church, the Jewish center became the elementary school, and the kosher butcher became the grocery.

The Torah this Rabbi found for me had been stuffed in the staircase of a building he thinks used to house the synagogue. It wasn't just the Torah from the town of my ancestors, but from the building where my grandfather likely had his bar mitzvah. It wasn't just the Torah from the same room where my grandfather and my great-grandparents sat and prayed. It wasn't just the four walls where cousins who may have looked like me sat in pews, separated by gender, genuflecting to the words and tunes that now escape my mouth.

No, it was more than that.

These were the scrolls that my family read from. The dust on these pages came from their clothes a hundred years ago. There was a *yad*, a pointer, they found in a back closet. A long silver stick with a molded hand at the top and a finger which helps the reader follow in the ancient scrolls, because humans aren't supposed to touch the sacred manuscript.

So this pointer that they found just a few feet from the half-destroyed Torah most likely had my grandfather's fingerprints on it, the Rabbi said.

When I heard these were discovered, the town came alive and I needed to see this place I'd rarely thought of. So I booked the flight from Detroit to New York, to Minsk, the train to Brest, the car to Pinsk, the bus to the small town nobody has ever heard of, to touch my past.

The Rabbi who found and repaired the Torah, the same man who found the yad and held it before my eyes with surgical gloves so as not to smear my grandfather's DNA, led the way. His enthusiasm for the place, the story and the history were only topped by my father's eyes as he listened to the tale of the discovery. He sat by my father's bed and told him this story with all the emotion of a Talmudic scholar:

"Walking through the church, the floorboards creaked, and the walls seemed to shake in the wind," the Rabbi said. "No one knew how old the actual structure was because all the town records were destroyed. No one thought the building would survive the demolition of a people."

"The floors were weak and at a point it felt unsafe. So I walked the final steps alone. I walked up to the proscenium, as they now called it, holding the railing which provided little support. I was being very deliberate with my steps; something about the place felt unsteady. I dragged my feet up, but in my earnestness to get my foot to the next level, the toe of my right boot smashed through the front of the final step."

"The thin wood shattered as if it were glass," he said. "I looked behind me at my hosts, worried about the damage I had caused, about the repair on this ancient step before Sunday services would commence in a few hours."

"So I got down on one knee, knowing my long black coat would pick up the dust from the floor and whatever was under the floorboard," the Rabbi said. "I turned on the flashlight from my phone and I surveyed the damage."

"But it wasn't the hole in that step that caught my eye. I saw something soft inside. At first I thought it was an animal, a rodent maybe. But something compelled me to reach for it, even into the dark space that had been dark for so many years. And I felt the feeling of cloth that I had held in my arms before. It was the feeling of a Torah scroll, the feeling of the dressing of the Torah that I carry around our synagogue every week. And I knew I had discovered the past."

All of us who heard the story were rapt. We knew the touch of that velvet he felt inside that dark hole, inside that darkening synagogue. We could picture how he pulled out that small Torah, the one that had been touched by my grand-relatives and all those faces in all those pictures on all those walls.

And now I was on a plane to see this place. With Rabbi sitting just a few rows ahead of me, my mind swirled of possibilities of what I might find. I was on my way to not just this place, but to walk across the bimah that had played such a central role in the stories of my youth. The stories my grandfather told me, the ones passed down to my father that were woven somehow into my imagination along with the stage productions of *Fiddler* and *The Diary of Anne Frank,* which were staples of my childhood.

My father's stroke precipitated my trip. I did not want to wait another year. I wanted to come back with stories that could spark his imagination about a time and a place he felt closer to than I did.

The day I arrived in the town was rainy and cold, which is just as I suspected it would be. Nineteen twenties Russia in black-and-white pictures always suggested cold and wet, and here I was in a town with fewer buildings than I imagined, but it was as dark as the photos in that poorly lit hallway in my grandmother's apartment.

When I approached the building, it seemed sturdier. It wasn't a working church as I thought I had heard, but it felt like a religious structure without any overtly religious décor. There was a woman who kept saying the word "church," her only English word, but now the building appeared to be used mostly for storing boxes, crates and empty wood pallets.

I asked if I could go inside, and she indicated she would have to find a light, which I think meant the fuse box, because when she unlocked the door, she headed to the basement, and when she came back there was a small light that hung above where the ark might have been. It was a single bulb hanging from a long cord, but it didn't move or sway as I had pictured; it just sat there in its sixty-watt dullness, and I could see the dust mites hanging on for dear life.

The room, which is all it was, one large dark room, smelled of must and mold, again as I'd suspected. I shivered for a moment, maybe because it was cold and rain had started to fall, but more because I think I felt the presence of my family, the people whose nose I had, the ones whose hairline mine resembled, but whose voices I had never heard.

But in that room, all the noise being sucked out by the old wood and the lack of light, I felt my history in a way I hadn't before. The black-and-whites became color, the voices turned loud, and for the first time I could smell them. Their heavy coats on Shabbat morning, their breath as we neared the end of prayers, the snuff they would take at high holiday services to stay awake, the weight of their hands on mine as I tried to stand for the Amidah at the end of a long day.

I approached the bimah with caution, remembering the words of the Rabbi, the frailty of the steps, the wobbliness of the railing. But I did not hear the creaks he spoke of. The wood flooring did not match the dark wood of the walls; instead it was lighter, newer, as if it had been replaced in the intervening years.

The railing, which wobbled so much in the story, seemed firm, with a fake wood that was splinter-free, smoothly leading me toward the place of worship.

There were five steps to the bimah, and halfway up I knelt down to feel the flooring, looking for the place where the Rabbi's foot entered, the place where the Torah hid for all these years, the place where maybe, just maybe, a relative of mine had stuffed the small scrolls, as the Nazis broke down the door before turning them into memories.

But the floor was solid, almost like linoleum. There was no place for a foot to penetrate and no stain from where a foot had gone through. No opening, no decay, no remnant.

Once I reached the top and looked out, I was no longer a fifty-year-old man in search of his history. I was that thirteen-year-old boy who was weeks from being sent to the States to live with his cousins until the war was over. I was the father of the bar mitzvah as he chanted, and I spoke words to him in Russian or in Yiddish or in Hebrew. And I looked up into the balcony to see where my great-grandmother would have sat with her sisters, all fat faces from the photos, all burned in the fires.

And I cried.

The old woman who had let me in that day, the one I bribed to find a key to open the door, sat in the pew, unmoved, watching me. I figured she had seen dozens of foreign men come to this place to reclaim some memory, to memorialize the lives of the people they'd never met.

This stale old building with the refurbished floors and railings that she walked by each day, the building which to her was simply a place where she might get out of the rain or the cold. A building which for her was a source of income, a way for her to make a few dollars, which still went a long way.

I imagined she would stand and watch the men, and sometimes women, walk the length of the building looking for ghosts and asking questions in a language she did not know.

So when I was done crying, feeling empty of tears, but full of memories, I placed a twenty-dollar bill in her hand, and I walked into the cold street that had turned muddy.

I retraced my steps, the bus to the car to the train to the big city where I returned to my hotel. Eight hours had passed, but I had traversed centuries. But the Rabbi was gone. He was too sick to come with me that day, but when I returned, a man at the front desk said he had checked out; his only message was that our flight was on time for the following morning and we would reconnect once back home.

"There are some exciting discoveries in another part of the country, and I am off to find more history," the note said.

I dined alone that night in the hotel lobby, although I felt as if I were at the biggest family reunion. I spoke with my father about all that I had seen, the pictures I had sent. I must have stood out eating the schnitzel special at the hotel restaurant, white pods in my ears, speaking too loudly in English to a family across the ocean. But I didn't care because I felt something that day that I had never felt before and in the intervening years have yet to feel again. It was the connection to a larger narrative, not just about my people but about myself.

It was the story going back more than a century, a story that included me in it. My story always started in the 1970s, and I could go through the decades and remember dates and songs and people and homes I'd lived in and schools I attended and jobs I'd had.

Addresses, phone numbers, BlackBerrys, flip phones and iPhones, movies, television shows, and aol.com accounts. But now my story went further back. And I could dive into a world I'd previously only seen as scattered scenes and pictures.

Like pieces of a puzzle, they now formed a clear picture and a narrative that previously didn't exist. It was like being told the words to a song that you once thought was instrumental.

I sat alone on the flight home.

I thought about where the Rabbi might be. Could his discovery in another town be as miraculous and meaningful as mine had been? And so I let it be. Yes, it was my trip and I had paid for his flight and his rental car, the hotel, his meals and "incidentals," along with the $25,000 price for the Torah, once he made it kosher by cleaning it up, as well as a $10,000 contribution to his "Save the Torah" foundation.

What price history? What price family?

I never saw the Rabbi again, except for his picture in the paper on the day of his sentencing.

He was indeed finding his next adventure, another fake story in a real setting.

He'd gone to the cities; he'd been to the camps. His description of the places was impeccable. The beggar outside, the weather, the cost, the trek to get there. And he could conjure stories in these far-off places, because he knew that even if someone was crazy enough to retrace the steps, he controlled the details, telling people what happened because there was no one to verify.

What kind of idiot takes a plane, a bus, a train to some smelly back lot of a town where the people are as inhospitable as the climate? Imagine a place where the townspeople know their only visitors come because of some ancestral atrocities.

And so he would go and find the place and take the story from there, because no one would ever know; there was nothing to certify.

I didn't tell my father before he died.

It would be years until I admitted it myself and even more before I told my wife.

They hadn't seen the story in the papers. By then my father's eyesight was so bad he couldn't read. And it wouldn't have been a story my wife would have noticed. I'm not even sure she knew the name of the Rabbi.

In court he argued for leniency by telling the judge that he was reconnecting Jews with their heritage, even if "parts of it weren't exactly true."

"Do you believe every passage of the Torah just as it's written?" the Rabbi asked rhetorically to the judge, the jury, and the universe.

"You are a Rabbi," the judge said. "How can you not believe?"

"I believe in the long narrative," he said. "I believe in believing. My stories served a purpose, they filled a need. They provided hope. They were the next chapter in our people's story."

They still got him on tax evasion, wire and mail fraud. He served four years. I can petition the court to get my money back.

But I got what I paid for.

# Chargeback

*This story came to me on a drive back from Rehoboth Beach Delaware. I was driving down Route 16, past the outdoor mall around Milton and Ellendale and I thought about the robbery. I pulled over and scribbled. The reason I like the story is that I think there are many ways to go with it, but it morphed into a writer and her interest in characters. There was a longer version to this story, and there may be more to come.* Doubly Mad *bought it very quickly in March 2021 and published it in June. In July* Glint Literary Journal *accepted it as well.*

SHE FINALLY SAW A GUN UP CLOSE.

And it was such a relief.

The three-hour drive to and from the beach always required a stop—sciatica—just to walk it out, shake it a little, get things back into place.

A rest stop, a parking lot, the side of the road.

Tiny towns of less than a thousand people dot the spine of central Delaware.

She stopped in a deserted parking lot and was about to stretch when she saw the gun so close she could smell it. The metal and the ridges around the barrel were so clear she could see where a bullet made its mark.

She felt like a fraud, writing about these things she'd never seen, never held. And now a gift.

The quarantine had shut her down; she was unable to finish anything and get it right. It always surprised her how many books and movies were written where guns and knives made star appearances. Shots and deaths of all sorts played center stage, yet the author likely had never seen anybody die, other than an odd grandparent in an antiseptic hospital room.

Following Chekhov's refrain that if a pistol is visible in Act I, it better go off in Act III. For her it was sitting in a drawer unable to catch.

So when he pulled it from his jacket, she was focused on its size, how it fit into his hand, the marks, how dirty it was.

"Give me your purse," he said.

"You need a nurse?" she asked. A coronavirus mask over his face made him hard to understand.

"Purse, your purse," he said, lifting a cheap imitation surgical mask.

"Not my purse, please," she said.

"Just your money," he said.

Normally there would be a wad of twenties in her leather wallet, but she stopped carrying cash a few months earlier.

"I have nothing," she said.

She could feel him looking at her Mercedes, her purse with a fancy logo, her bone-white sneakers.

"I mean, I don't carry cash anymore," she said. "You know, the pandemic."

She reached into her purse and pulled out a handful of credit cards, receipts, tissues, wipes, and stray tampons (her daughter's).

"Gimme a credit card," he said.

"What?" she asked, pulling it out with her thumb.

"No, not the American Express," he said.

"What are you going to do with it?" she asked, reaching for a Visa card, her forehead crinkling with questions.

Her heart slowed and the conversation took on a tone of a customer and vendor who didn't accept cash.

"Don't report it" were his last words before he ran off.

"But you're not me," she said, unaware of how stolen credit cards work.

She looked at the empty parking lot and was struck by the quiet. There was nobody, as if all the stores closed at that moment. She couldn't wait to get home.

"How was the drive?" her husband asked when she walked in from the garage. He was leaning over the sink with a full peach dripping from his hands.

"Fine," she said, hurrying into her den.

She logged into her online banking. But in the two hours since the crime, the credit card was unused.

Since she did the bills, there was no one to notice the extra odd charges that might follow.

But why didn't she just cancel it, she wondered.

The following morning she logged in again to witness the crime. She was looking for a television; wasn't it always a television or some big electronics? A car maybe, video games, something outlandish that she would never buy. Something to trip the credit card company so they might call and she could lie to them, and her husband, and say she hadn't noticed the missing card; maybe she'd left it at a store and someone swiped it.

She would need a story for why she didn't notice the missing card.

"So they took just this one credit card?" her husband, the stickler, might ask.

According to her online banking account, the most recent charge was the gas station from just before she left. Wait, there was a new charge. Forty-nine dollars and eighty-five cents at a place she'd never heard of with the words Fried Chicken in the name.

She searched and found it, just a few miles from the parking lot where she was robbed.

She looked at the menu online. Everything was so reasonably priced. She tried to figure out what he might have ordered to rack up almost fifty dollars.

It looked like dinner.

She spent hours on the restaurant website looking at the pictures. Who was this guy and who did he eat with? She examined the photos taken by other diners; she couldn't imagine this is what people bought with stolen credit cards. A bucket of chicken, biscuits, and iced tea?

That night she couldn't sleep. She thought about this young man who waved a loaded pistol in her face so he could buy dinner.

She spent the following day in one of her most productive writing jags in months. It was exhilarating and exhausting.

Later she went back to her bank account, and there were more orders, and she couldn't wait to live them. But she was disappointed by the ordinariness of it all.

The thief spent less than twenty-five dollars at a Walgreens? The kind of order her college-age child might make and she wouldn't even notice.

She called the credit card company and asked for details on the order, claiming she didn't remember going. The operator read through the items: toilet paper and toothpaste, compression socks and aspirin.

Again she did nothing.

This became her ritual. Each day as she sipped her morning coffee with a dash of sugar-free vanilla, but before her writing, she would check the orders, looking up the stores where he was shopping, analyze the purchases, and try desperately to draw conclusions about what she was paying for.

It moved from a crime to a partnership. Where they ate, what they ordered, and how they lived.

One morning two weeks into this crime spree, she froze. The orders were traveling. A gas station in Delaware, a McDonald's in Washington, DC. He was coming after her. He found out where she lived and now for some reason he was coming for more, maybe for cash. He must have assumed that anyone who didn't cancel a credit card and was willing to pay for someone else's life had so much extra money that surely there was more.

And what would her defense be when this man showed up at her front door?

He'd been using her credit card for weeks. What to say when the police, or her husband, inevitably ask: "Didn't you see the unrecognized charges?" "Why didn't you cancel the card?" "Why didn't you call the credit card company?"

"How rich are you?"

She sat at the computer, staring at the blue screen in fear, then looking out the window as a neighbor filled up their aboveground pool. It had become all the rage in these neighborhoods during the pandemic.

"Trash," she said under her breath.

But why was he coming after her? He was getting away with it. She was letting him and now he was going to literally bite the hand that fed him.

But he must have wondered as well. When was this sword coming down on him?

Maybe he worried every time he went into a store that it would be the last time. The police would be there waiting for him, and they were gonna kill him like all the others. Maybe the card would get rejected on a website, and one day, guns drawn, they would show up at his door instead of a brown corrugated box?

Every hour she checked online. Sometimes twice an hour, like tracking a package from stop to stop. But then the orders bypassed her, moving south from Delaware to a sub shop in Roanoke, a rib shack in Knoxville, and gas stations in between. But what consistently struck her was the moderation of the things he bought and the things he didn't buy. There were no thousand-dollar meals, no binge buying.

At her desk, unable to finish the story she was writing, she'd Google the names and places and watch where he stayed and what he did. Maybe he was afraid that a big wasteful purchase would ring some bells and force her to cancel the card and decline the purchases. But didn't he know it was fear that drove her too? She wouldn't have cancelled that card, he knew where she lived, he had all her details.

Ellen asked herself was it fear or fascination or simple voyeurism?

She rationalized that it was okay to get a little insight for a story she might write, a look inside his life. "I mean, I'm paying for it."

But he didn't show up at her door, and the orders just stopped.

For days she was stuck, sitting at her computer in silence. The dogs milled about, her husband in his office, the house empty, the kids hadn't called in a week. She knew so little about their lives anymore, but so much about this man, and now he'd gone dark.

In real life too many of her questions were answered with one word or a description that her family assumed would pacify her, but didn't. She needed more. She needed to know not just that her son had a date, but who was it with, where did they go, what did they eat, the color of the tablecloth?

By now nobody in her family wanted to end up a character in her books and so she got nothing.

Her coffee got cold.

Her mood turned dark. No food, no dinner, no gas, no motel?

Where were they? Did they find another source of income? Did something happen in Knoxville?

Did he rob someone else? Why would he leave her when he had this source and it was working? She wanted to call somebody, trace the card, find out where they were. But she had no connection. It only went one way. His shopping was her breadcrumbs. And although it was her money, he held the crust.

"What's with you?" her husband asked.

"Nothing," she said without looking up from her computer.

He paused for a moment and then left the room.

After a week without a purchase, she searched the newspapers in Knoxville and then the nearby towns, watching the local news, looking for a familiar face. Was there a death, a car accident, a family who died from a gas leak?

Nothing.

She was tempted to cancel the card.

Maybe that would smoke him out.

*If he's not gonna use it, then I'm gonna cancel it and then he'll see.*

As a writer she would spend her pre-pandemic days in coffee houses and restaurants like the writers of old who watched people at night and then wrote about them during the day. Then quarantine hit, and her usual places were locked up, and her husband and children clammed up.

She needed to watch the world to make up the stories from the snippets they told. But in quarantine she had no way in. Even if she went out, there was nobody, and so she sat at home and tried to imagine, and nothing came. Until she saw the gun.

Now she'd learned enough from the scraps of carryout, the daily sundry purchases to outline her stories.

After five months of quarantine, she was back in, and now he was trying to take it away. She needed to see how the story ended.

The weather turned and they were done with the beach for the season.

She made an excuse to go back.

She left in the morning and drove with uncommon speed toward the mall parking lot where she had been robbed.

She parked at the far end of the lot and waited.

The sun rose to the middle of sky, and she went into the 7-Eleven to get a large coffee. She dumped the coffee outside the car and used it as her bathroom.

The hours passed and she worried whether he was in Knoxville or DC or at her front door.

As the sky darkened she sat upright and watched as he crossed the empty lot.

She pulled the car toward him, too quickly for an unfamiliar parking lot in the dark, until her left front tire rolled up on the parking block, stopping the car, the sound of scraping metal stunning him.

The wheel was elevated as she flung open the door, her feet dangling above the ground. She made the jump and ran toward him.

"You, you there, wait," she yelled, the young man now bathed in her headlights.

He looked around as if he were about to run.

"Why aren't you using it?" she asked.

He looked at her with a look between fear and wonder.

"What?"

"You stopped using my card," she said.

The man looked around the desolate parking lot.

"I don't know what you're talking about," he said.

"You stole my credit card," she said. "I gave you my card and then I was worried."

"Worried?"

"That something happened to you," she said.

"What?"

"In Knoxville," she said.

"I cancelled it," he said.

"You what?" she asked.

"I didn't need it," he said.

"But," she started.

"I got my old job back," he said.

"Oh, you did," she said, feeling deflated and foolish. "You're not a thief?"

"I was out of work," he said.

"But you had a gun."

"It wasn't real," he said.

Lights flashed and sirens rang as a single car pulled toward them. A young police officer emerged, his hand on his holster.

"It's fine, Officer," she blurted.

"What's going on here," he asked, approaching the elevated car.

"I hit this barrier," she said, "and this man ran out to help me."

"Do you need a tow?" the police officer asked.

"I think I might," she said.

"We'll get you fixed right quick," the officer said, tugging at his phone.

"Thank you," she said to the thief, who said nothing and hurried away toward the alley behind the mall.

"So what happened here?" the officer asked.

"Just an old woman missing something that's right in front of her," she said.

"We're seeing a lot of that, ma'am," the police officer said.

# Talking Windows

*This story waited the longest to see the light of day. I wrote it in 2015 under a different name,* Watching Windows, *but never found an audience. Not enough seemed to happen. And so I decided to take all the stories that hadn't been accepted and turn them into flash fiction, basically cutting them down to 1,000 words. And once I did the* Otherwise Engaged Literary and Arts Journal *published it in the summer of 2021. I had the pleasure of buying the hard copy off Amazon, which I was more than glad to do. This is the longer version, about 3,000 words.*

IT WAS NOT A MOVIE SHE'D WANT TO SEE ANYWAY.

She would have called it "artsy" because Tom Cruise wasn't in it. At least that's what he told himself.

The movie theatre was nearly empty when he arrived just before noon on a Tuesday. A cluster of old people; the man of the group sitting on the aisle, two canes dangling from his walker. Separately a pair of middle-aged women, who seemed to be hiding like Kevin, sat close to the screen. There was another errant single who came late and left early.

The exhilaration came from knowing how careful he'd been earlier in the day: purchasing the ticket, using a different email account, avoiding the joint credit card, parking in an unusual spot at the office so no one would see his car disappear. But then there was the pain of knowing he would blow it. At some point, maybe days or weeks later, they would be at dinner with friends and somebody would say, "Have you seen *Dark House*? It won the big award at Sundance." And he would blurt something out, eager to add to the conversation and remember, a moment too late, that it was his secret to keep.

And maybe she would miss it too, for a bit, but then something would give him away, the clipped way he spoke or how his ears burned red. And then later that night, when they got into bed, or when his mouth was full of toothpaste, she'd slip it in. And he'd try to deny it, or say he'd read the review or seen the trailer and that was all. Did she even care, really? The little lies upon which their marriage was built didn't matter. Didn't everybody have the movie they snuck into, or the day they played hooky, the time they didn't follow the rules?

He had done nothing wrong. Or at least there were worse things one could do to a spouse, like the things she was doing.

He felt it buzz. Was it phantom or real? He closed his eyes and reached down his thigh. It was his phone. He pulled it from his pocket, she was calling. How did he forget to turn it off? Besides, he never gets a signal in this cave of a theatre. He couldn't pick up. Why is she calling? What if it's an emergency? But if he picks up and can't hear he'll have to leave and call her back. He let it ring until it went to voicemail, and then stuffed it deep into the furry pocket of his jacket and pushed it under his left butt cheek and sat on it for the rest of the movie.

Two hours and seven minutes later he remained seated, jacket collar up around his ears, waiting for everyone to leave. The high school kid was already sweeping up the popcorn between the seats before the lights went on and the train of old folks struggled to clear their aisle. Kevin pretended he was watching the credits with some level of interest. Maybe looking for his own name he knew wasn't there.

Finally he had to leave and head out into the cold. The strong sunshine of the January day where the glare off the snow made him put on sunglasses. He wrapped his old gray scarf around his mouth as he walked past the Starbucks to the Tastee Diner up on the main road.

He liked to sit at the counter, but didn't want to risk the exposure, so he took a booth in the corner and sat facing away from the door. He never fully examined what he feared, what exposure was. Seeing a friend? It was unlikely. Seeing a woman from his wife's orbit perhaps was the real pain point. Cornered with no way to explain it. Explain what? People don't take breaks anymore.

But he was the hunter and didn't want to be hunted. He was looking for something he knew he would find. Could there be anything worse than being found out.

"Black coffee and a piece of pie," he told the waitress.

"Apple or cherry?" she asked.

It didn't matter. "Apple," he said. She wasn't paying attention anyway, barely making eye contact. He didn't care, he just wanted his coffee and his notebook and the ability to decode the secret across the street.

His reporter's notebook was long and thin, like his wife, nine inches by four, the ones that line his desk drawer at work, at home, and in places where he hides the writing he didn't want anyone to see, but secretly wished someone would discover.

He would run out of notebooks, but never out of words.

He scanned the room for a story.

The windowsill, smudges of ketchup, and breadcrumbs creating an obstacle course for the ants that come inside from the cold. How did they get there, those stains; who was the child who squeezed the ketchup, or the lonely lady sitting with her biscuit, crumbs absently falling from her hands and chin?

The shingles that hung over the roof, the bricks across the way, the mortar that oozed out like frosting. All placed there on purpose or by accident by people whose work now went unnoticed. These are the nooks where he searched for stories; these are the things that spoke to him, that whispered the words he had hoped would fill bookshelves in homes, not binders in his drawers.

The ceiling tiles, the corner of the booth, the crust of the pie, the store across the way.

Now he looked past the window to see a woman his age, maybe forty-five, all red-faced and sweaty, coming out of the yoga studio. But maybe she didn't come from a yoga class. *She's sleeping with the yogi master. He could check the schedule; maybe there are no classes at this time. It didn't matter, it was his story; she went there every day at three o'clock, telling her husband and the nanny, and instead of sweating for an hour doing yoga, she's sweating for ten minutes doing something else.*

Passing her in the opposite direction is a woman in her mid-twenties pushing a stroller with the newborn tucked and swaddled. *But it isn't hers. She just swiped it from her husband's ex-girlfriend. She's taking it to get a blood test and see if it matches.* There are no bad ideas, he thought, and kept writing.

Turning his head, he saw the waitress sitting at the counter on one of the red stools with the silver base that looks like a giant mushroom. He could hear her filing her nails and he wanted to scream as every waitress cliché came into his head, and he wrote them down: She wants to be an actress, she is married to the owner, she was a model, she was on the streets.

But the motherlode was always the large two-story Barnes and Noble that stood tall across the street, filled with people going in and out. The door acted as a dividing line for those anticipating the warmth of the store and those preparing for the cold to come. Are they visitors or buyers? When did it become okay to spend your day at a store without buying? Looking up at the second floor, the world of the bookstore coffee shop is brought to life. All the tables near the window are filled with people and laptops, tied together in a web of plugs and cords.

A series of small tables, big enough for one chair on either side, line the walls of the four-paneled bay windows extending out from the building. *There is a story in those windows,* he knew one would arrive, but he'd hoped it would be something new. Every Wednesday he would see the same story and it haunted him the rest of the week.

In window number one was his second greatest fear, the unemployed fifty-ish man who still called his hair salt-and-pepper. But even from this distance Kevin knew it was white, slicked back with product, too spiky for a man his age. *His day started so positive,* Kevin wrote, *filling his coffee while the laptop booted up. Saving his food purchase, maybe a fruit cup, until closer to ten-thirty. And then he reached for his coffee only to realize it was empty, but it was too early to get his second cup, preferring to wait until lunch. Too much too early draws war with his bladder, which fights back, unleashing a stream of urinating sessions that disrupts any momentum. Sometimes he welcomed the break when the only thing moving was his body.*

By the time Kevin spied him, his desk was littered with the day's frustrations: muffin wrappers, a half-eaten sandwich, and he was no longer job-searching, but killing time, mostly on websites where the volume needs to be turned all the way down.

The waitress finally comes back from ignoring him with his piece of pie and black coffee. He looked up to thank her, but she was gone before the sound of the plate clanking the Formica hit his ears. He lifted the mug to smell the coffee, test its strength and its heat. He put it down; it was almost time for the real show.

In the next window, four girls, all jammed around the small table. Not more than fifteen years old, although Kevin was better at guessing those in middle-age than in middle-school. Maybe high school freshmen? Probably the same age as his son Jeffrey. In the center was a large drink masquerading as coffee, but all he could imagine was whipped cream oozing out of the top, and the darkness that is more likely solid brownie than liquid. The girls were laughing as they passed the drink from mouth to mouth. One straw. But they don't seem to care; they are using this nine-thousand-calorie drink to wash down the two wilting croissants dripping with butter. They look respectful, leaning in, talking in low tones. Not library-worthy, but bookstore-worthy, secretive? *What is it about books that makes people go hush?* Kevin wrote.

They kept lowering their heads, craning their necks like birds to eat, and then they'd share a morsel of gossip and their bodies flared back as they covered their mouths. Maybe they are just happy kids because the semester is almost over. Maybe there's a dance this weekend and they all just got asked. Maybe none of them got asked and they are commiserating. No, they look too happy, too hip, too cute. Maybe they're all making a suicide pact, and this is their final meal?

Kevin scribbled faster and faster because maybe in their backpacks, next to the eyeliner and puffy pens with feathers on top, are pounds of explosives, and they are going to all get up in a minute, run down the escalator, out the front door, and *ka-boom*, the place will go up in a million tiny shreds of unread books.

Next to them is an old woman who shouldn't be out in this kind of weather. A web of unkempt white hair she goes every week to the beauty parlor and gets all dolled up, Kevin imagined. She reminded him of his mother before Alzheimer's took her. She was always so well-kept until the end when he'd come visit and her hair was askew, and her makeup mismatched and smudged and he knew it was no longer his mom. He didn't visit her for the last two years. His brother called on a Tuesday to tell him she was gone.

The woman in the window is small and sitting hunched over her small cup of coffee in a long powder-blue woolen coat. She takes small sips, but Kevin can see it's too hot for her. She holds the cup with both hands, warming her bony body.

She looks over at the girls and watches them laugh. Kevin wonders what she thinks. *Is she envious of these kids and their carefree day? Maybe that was her childhood too. Maybe she is resentful of those little shits sitting in here spending ten dollars on these candy drinks, when she only spends ten dollars a day on all her groceries. Or maybe she's onto them. She is the spy the CIA sent and she's been tracking these Al-Qaeda brats for months and she's about to save the town from the dirty bomb in their backpacks.*

In the final window is a woman he knows too well, with curly hair that frames her face, and a set of eyes and lips that Kevin knows almost better than his own. She is standing, scanning the street while a cup that he knows is filled with mint tea sits on the ledge, along with her elbows. He knows her routine.

When she appears his stomach churns and his pen no longer writes. He can't find the words when she is in view, because he knows what happens next and it breaks his heart every time.

The man enters the store from below and she remains facing the window as if she doesn't see him. But Kevin knows, as well as she, that he is coming. She will close her eyes as he approaches from behind with his own cup of something. And then the two of them will sit and talk. Kevin doesn't know what they are saying and can't seem to make up a story for this couple. It hurts too much to watch her listen to him with an intensity he thought she had lost over the years. Her eyes never leave this bearded man as they absently pick at pieces from inside a muffin. With his beard and her mane of curly hair, he imagined their faces melded together, their children looking like dandelions.

Why does she meet this man, and where do they go? Kevin lies about movies and she lies about muffins; what's the difference? He is alone and she is not. Is that by choice? If he found someone to join him in his clandestine movie time would it be different? What if the waitress offered to sit with him, part of the service? And she sat with him telling her sad tale and he wrote it down. What if she used his fork to pick at the fruit chunks inside his pie? Would that be the same?

It sounded like a good idea when he started working with his wife, six years ago. At least that's what he told people when he hadn't worked for nine months. But it didn't sound so good anymore. How could working for his wife sound like a good idea he asked himself in quiet moments. How could the progression from running a marketing department with ten direct reports to selling your wife's perfumed soaps, be called progress on anyone's scale? It was supposed to be a bridge, not a destination. He had no choices back then. Fewer now.

What bothered him about watching his wife talk to the other man was that when he lied she didn't care. This idea that a strong marriage is built on a stack of white lies didn't work for him. He wanted to know everything. He couldn't take the not knowing, but now that he knew it, he didn't like that either.

"I'm not going to couples therapy," she said a month before, when he brought home a name he had gotten from a friend.

"It's not couples' therapy, it's my therapy, and you're just coming along for the ride," he said.

At this point she stopped what she was doing and with an honesty and clarity he couldn't ignore said: "I know there are things that we could fix," she said. "But I don't want to."

"Why not make it better?"

"Because it's not that bad," she said. "I know we both make accommodations, I know there are reactions that I bury, I know there are things I don't know. But I don't want to dig in and unpack all this."

"Why hold all this in?" he said.

"I don't want some therapist telling me how unhappy I am by telling me how happy I could be," she said. "I'm happy enough, and the discovery of more unhappiness isn't worth it."

"I need someone to talk to," he said.

"I have friends," she said. "Friends who don't tell me I've been burying this stuff for eighteen years, and now let's shed some light on all the coping mechanisms we've developed."

She exhaled deeply and looked away into the darkened window of their kitchen.

"I like my coping mechanisms; they work. For me"

"But they don't for me," he said into the mirror when he was alone again in the bathroom, too quiet for anyone to hear.

His wife didn't care about his indiscretions, as long as he didn't bring them home.

Instead of women or strip clubs, his secret was afternoon movies and hidden journaling.

In their life of work and home, family and friends, there was no space for him. The mornings were a rush of breakfast and carpool where he was treated like the employee he was, filling in when she had something "important" to do. At night, he slipped too quickly into his glass of Merlot or the shot of Tequila he might drop in the dark of the basement.

Nothing else gets written in his notebook that day. Pages of questions without answers, escapades without proof, worry with only his imagination to guide him.

Without taking his eyes off his wife he reaches for his coffee and puts it to his lips. "Goddamnit," he mutters; it's cold.

He looks at the waitress, and then back to the windows, but his wife is gone. He pushes the fat white mug and pie plate away and closes the notebook. He's out of words. The story is over.

# Winning Numbers

*So much of the past year I spent thinking about the nature of luck, timing, placement. I tried to explore it with this story: What does it mean to have luck, to feel you don't have it, and to what end. I finished this in the summer of 2021 and it was accepted by* Front Porch Review *for its October issue. I like the discussion the characters are having and how they all interpret luck differently. I fiddled with the ending a dozen times.*

WHAT'S THE FIRST THING YOU WOULD DO IF YOU WON A MILLION dollars?

It wasn't a question Ray asked or answered. Which was surprising for a guy who played the numbers five days a week.

So when $850,000 showed up in their bank account—because you always take the lump sum, never the 15-year payout—he only wanted to spend it as fast as he could.

At first he and his wife, Marti, did all the things expected by their friends. He bought stupid shit like a Jet Ski, even though they didn't live near water. She bought matching sweatsuits for a family reunion that wasn't planned. He got a new Ford F-150. And for a full week, they went out for lobster every night.

But the restlessness that drove him to Rick's Liquor to buy those tickets each day of the week was still there. The unease of life that pushed him off the road to stop for "just a couple of beers" after lunch before getting behind the wheel. The incomplete feeling still settled inside of him even as the money arrived and then began to dissipate.

Marti mostly bought things for her family, helped her sisters with the groceries, didn't skimp on the Little Debbies anymore. But after a couple of weeks, she wanted more. Not more stuff, not more money, but more security. Isn't that what millionaires have?

"Maybe we should see one of them lawyers," she said to Ray. "One that's been callin'."

"You can call 'em all you want," Ray told her. "They just callin' for your money. They never called before."

"We didn't have no money before," she said.

"Exactly," he said.

Ray called their purchases "upgradin'." Just getting better stuff like new TVs and one of them speakers you can carry around the house.

But Marti was worried it would run out. "He's actin' like he's trying to spend it all," she told her sister Bonnie.

"He cain't spend a million dollars," Bonnie said.

But he was, Marti thought.

Ray also upped his spending on Lotto tickets from five a day to ten, then twenty, then one hundred, and by the time the Jet Ski arrived in the driveway, he was spending $500 a day on tickets.

"You ain't gonna win again," Rick would say to him when the line at Rick's Liquor got too long as they waited for the machine to spit up tickets, the *rat-tat-tat* of the machine drowning out the store noise and everyone else's patience. Soon the ink would blur and go blank, and Rick would open the top to change it while waiting customers groaned.

"I'm buyin' 'em," Ray would say, "it's your job to sell 'em. Now sell 'em."

"You ain't gonna win again is all I'm saying," Rick said, noticing the increase in spending.

Ray was pretty sure Rick was just sore because the winning ticket wasn't bought at Rick's but instead at the 7-Eleven down the street.

"Maybe if you'd hurry up, I wouldn't have to go someplace else to buy 'em," Ray said.

Rick focused on changing the ink in the machine. He knew too well that arguing with a man who was drunk before lunchtime was not a winning strategy for him or his business or the other customers in line.

"You know I ain't won nuthin' yet," Ray added. Just below the din of the machine.

Later that afternoon Ray woke to the angry sound of his wife's voice. "When you gonna quit?" Marti asked him when she found him asleep at the wheel of his new truck parked in their driveway.

He wiped the drool from his cheek and some that slipped down to the steering wheel where the word FORD was engraved and his saliva pooled.

"What time is it?" he asked. "The numbers been picked yet?"

"You always said if you ever won the Lotto, you would be quittin' work as soon as you could," she said. "And now you can."

"I cain't," he said, resting his head on his forearm.

"You can but you ain't," she said.

They all expected he would quit. All the guys who drove long haul back and forth to Pittsburgh. The guys he'd see at the bar or he'd meet at the lunch truck when he wasn't drinking at noon. They all said they'd walk away if they won, told him that's what they would do. But he didn't wanna quit. Not yet.

"What would you do?" he asked her with a sadness in his voice she didn't recognize. "Would you quit?"

"Why are you still playing the Lotto?" she asked. "We already won."

"I gotta win," he said quietly.

"But why are you doin' it?" she asked. "You play to win. Winning is getting the money. You already got the money. So why are you playin'?"

He knew the best part of his day was going to Rick's and buying them tickets. And then, of course, the waiting. Waiting to see if he'd won, 'til the numbers were announced later that night. And maybe he was close, only a couple numbers off, and like a good golf shot, that morsel of good news propelled him to the next day, maybe encouraged a change of strategy, alter the numbers, vary the last one.

He couldn't give that up.

She'd just been lucky.

Later that night, sitting at the kitchen table, Marti yelled into the next room: "How many tickets you buyin'?"

The television was screaming at a volume that was not meant to hear the show as much as it was to drown her out.

"Five hundred," he said too quietly for her to hear. "And maybe more tomorrow."

"You're in early," Rick said the following day when Ray walked through the door just after ten in the morning. Ray usually came in later, smelling like he just finished the six-pack he'd started at lunch.

"Feelin' lucky," Ray said.

"It's better now," Rick said. "The morning is better because it's quiet, and no one needs to wait for Bertha to spit out your five hundred tickets."

"I'm glad it works for you," Ray said.

While Bertha the ticket machine belched out tickets, Rick rang him up.

"You gettin' beer too?" Rick asked. "I know it's a little early."

"Hell yeah, I'm getting beer. Ever heard of ice?" Ray said.

"Fine," Rick said and he punched at the cash register.

Ray plugged his card into the reader.

A moment later he grabbed it back, and just as he was putting it in his wallet, a sound came from the machine as a warning, not a welcome.

"What the hell, Ray?" Rick said.

"What?" he answered.

"Put the card back," Rick said.

Again he stuck it in the machine, fiddled a little with it, but the same warning buzzed out.

"Your card don't work," Rick said.

"Unless you charged me a million bucks, then it works," Ray said.

"It don't work," Rick said.

"It's your machine," Ray said.

"It says you're out of money," Rick said.

"Jesus Christ, Rick, you want me to start buying my tickets at the 7-Eleven too?" he said. "It's luckier over there."

"Try it again," Ray said.

But after another try and another, it still didn't work.

"You know I'm good for it," Ray said.

Rick nodded slowly.

"Don't I deserve a break?" Ray asked. "I just need a break."

"You're a millionaire," Rick said.

"You know that ain't mine," Ray said. "I didn't earn it."

"Who earns it?" Rick said. "Your wife was just lucky. And if your number comes up, it's because you were lucky too."

"So I'm not lucky," Ray said.

"It's not a game of skill," Rick said. "Life is not a game of skill, that's all I'm saying."

"But I deserve to win," Ray said. "I deserve it so much more than she does."

"We all know that," Rick said.

"And that's what makes me so sad, I mean mad," Ray said.

"You know I never do this, but I already printed 'em out, so. You can come back tomorrow and give me a new card or something," Rick said.

Rick's brother-in-law was sitting on a milk crate just behind the counter, flipping through a *Playboy*.

"Maybe ask your wife for some more of that money," the brother-in-law said without looking up from his reading.

Ray hadn't seen him. He looked around, confused, and then exploded, charging the brother-in-law, sending packs of gum and tiny flashlights flying off the counter.

Rick jumped in between them, pushing Ray back to the other side.

"Ray, you're a friend," Rick said. "Now come back tomorrow with the money."

Looking at his brother-in-law, Rick added, "And you shut the hell up."

Later that night Ray finished his beer in the car before walking into his house. He saw Marti's sister's car in the drive and decided he needed more beer in his blood before walking into an array of bags filled with girl junk. As he stumbled through the door, Marti yelled from the kitchen, "Is that you?"

He could hear Bonnie and Megan laughing in the other room, a jug of white zinfandel on the kitchen table.

"How was your night?" she asked, hoping he would follow her lead of cheerfulness.

He didn't look at them and kept shuffling.

"Hey, Ray," one or both of the sisters said.

But he stared straight into the living room, turning on the TV and turning up the volume.

Marti gave them a look and shook her head.

"Where's the money?" Ray shouted a moment later.

"You guys better go," Marti said softly.

"Where's the money?" he yelled again.

"What money?" she asked.

"The lottery money," he said.

"It's there," she said. "You know, in the bank."

"Well, it ain't because I couldn't get no money out," he said.

"Did you spend everything in your account already?" she asked.

With a flick of his finger, the television went silent.

"I didn't know I had a limit," he said, getting up from his chair.

"Everyone has a limit, hon," she said.

"I thought one mill was my limit," he said.

"Well, I don't think we want to spend it all," she said.

He looked into the kitchen. The table was filled with bags from Walmart, T-shirts and socks pouring out of them.

"You puttin' me on a budget?" he said. "I never put you on a budget."

"I always had a budget," she said. "A budget based on how much you made."

"And now I'm on a budget based on how much you made?" he shouted.

"We'd better go," one of the sisters said.

Marti's face dropped a little and then nodded as her sisters left. They gathered the bags from the table. Marti waited until they were out the front door before returning to meet Ray's glare.

"I don't want to run outta money," she said, now talking as loudly as he. "I don't wanna be poor."

"And the money I make made you poor?" he said.

"We spent everything you made," she said.

"You didn't make this Lotto money," he said. "You don't make more than me."

"I know I didn't, it's luck," she said.

"And you have it," he said.

"*We* have it," she said.

"I play it every goddam day and don't win nuthin'. You play once and you win the goddamn jackpot. You get the article in the paper. You get the big check," he said, his voice cracking.

"*We* get it," she said again.

"No, we don't," he said, slamming an empty beer can to the ground. "They all know I didn't win it. I get an allowance."

The following day Ray slept late. The sun was up and the room was midday lit when Marti found him sitting up and rubbing his temples.

"You still here?" she asked.

"What time is it?" he asked.

"You slept through your alarm," she said.

"I'm not goin' in," he said.

"Did ya quit?" she asked.

"Maybe now they'll fire me," he said.

"You don't want it to end like that," she said.

"They expectin' me to quit anyway," he said.

"Then go in and quit, but don't get fired for showin' up late," she said. "Don't leave on bad terms."

"They're my terms," he said, "so they ain't bad."

"If they fire you, it's their terms," she said. "You know why all those Lotto winners quit their jobs? Because it feels good."

He pounded his fist into the mattress before kicking his feet over the side of the bed and stomping into the bathroom.

The next time Marti saw him was in the basement of County Hospital.

She was at the grocery with her sisters when the call came in. She didn't recognize the number, but she thought maybe it was the lawyer she'd called earlier in the day, the one who the lottery people said she should talk to.

But it was the police at the hospital. They were the first ones on the scene. They couldn't trace the truck because it still had temporary plates, which got shredded from the fire hose and washed away.

She pieced together his last hour from three stories: Rick, the police chief, and Kishor at the 7-Eleven.

He had gone to Rick's, who wouldn't sell him more tickets because he still owed money from the previous day.

"Maybe *you* are the unlucky one," were the last words he said to Rick.

So he drove down to the 7-Eleven.

"He was drunk," Kishor said.

"How do you know that?" the police had asked.

"He said very mean things," Kishor said. "He yelled at us, he said we ruin his life. He wanted tickets but he had no money. I need money for the tickets, I told him."

"So he didn't buy any tickets?" Marti asked.

"I could not sell him tickets," Kishor said. "He did not have money."

"And then what?" the police had asked him.

Ray left the 7-Eleven, got into his new truck, and drove it with outsized force through the plate glass front of the store.

The police said they believed it was an accident.

"He put the car in drive instead of reverse," the policeman said.

It rammed through the front window of the store. The force sheared off the top of the truck, and the neon Budweiser sign crashed down into the car, electrocuting Ray again and again and again.

"I don't think he wanted to hurt me," Kishor said. "I think he just tried to leave. He was very drunk."

"I want to see the truck," Marti said.

They brought her to the dump where his truck lay, headless, the rain washing the inside.

She climbed into the front seat, shattered glass, debris from the store ceiling, and stacks of soggy Lotto tickets.

It was an accident, she told herself. No way he would ruin this new truck.

She found more tickets in the glove box and brought all the soiled tickets home and hung them from the shower with laundry clips.

When the numbers were drawn that night, she wrote them down and brought the paper into the bathroom, where she checked the hundreds of tickets.

Her heart pounded as she ticked them off, one then another, through the long lineup.

"Oh my God," she said quietly to herself. "He won."

Marti was halfway through the string of tickets when she found the winner. She carefully pulled the ticket from the stream and called her sister Bonnie to meet her at Rick's.

She pulled into the near-empty parking lot, tears filling her eyes. If he only knew, if only he knew.

"He won," she said, screaming as she ran up to her sister, waving the ticket in the air. "He won."

They hugged and now Bonnie cried too.

They went inside and told Rick he was gonna get a good payoff.

"Who won?" he asked, pouring them each a double whiskey from an open bottle he kept behind the counter.

"Ray won this time," she said.

Rick studied the ticket while they drank.

"You know I didn't sell him nuthin' today," Rick said.

"But this ticket was bought here, right?" Marti asked.

Slowly Rick looked up at the women, who'd already finished their drinks. "These tickets are from last month," he said. "These ain't winning numbers."

"They are," Marti said.

"These are old?" Bonnie said, looking at the date on the ticket.

"He lost," Rick said.

"He won," Marti said back at Rick.

"But the numbers are from the wrong day," he said. "Today's drawing can't match last month's ticket."

"He picked the winning number," she said.

"That ain't how it works," Rick said.

"How what works?" she said. "Luck? Luck only happens on a single day?"

"The Lotto," Bonnie said. "You cain't just bring in an old ticket and call it a winner."

"Yeah," Rick said. "It's a loser."

And then, looking at the two of them, she paused and took in a deep breath and said: "He died a winner, you hear? He picked the winning numbers. Luck don't happen on the day you decide. He hoped for it. He worked for it. He got it."

"That ain't how luck works," Rick said.

"Says who?" Marti said. "Says who?"

# She Said "Yes"

*In the summer of 2021 I took a Flash Fiction course at the Writer's Center in Bethesda and one of the exercises was about a story that goes in one direction and at some point you realize it's gone someplace else. Not quite* Sixth Sense, *but in that vein. I like the speed of it, it's still searching for a home.*

AND THAT WAS THE RIGHT ANSWER.

We learned in law school, and law television, not to ask a question unless you know the answer and I knew the answer because I was on deadline. If I didn't pop the question she would move out, walk out, run away from my life and the future we had been imagining. That's what she told me. She promised. She threatened. I believed her.

She said that by the time the flowers in the window box blossom she had better have a ring on that finger. And they were sprouting.

So at night I would sit in my big leather chair, the lone piece of furniture I salvaged from my bachelor days. It was stuffed in the corner, but I could still see out the window and watch the city go to bed. I could see families across the busy streets doing dishes, putting kids to bed, watching television together on the couch and I would wonder.

But I had fear. How do you know, I would ask my 27 year-old self, really know how you are going to feel about someone 50 years down the line? In my 20s all I was trying to do was get her into bed.

Her husband couldn't know how she would handle it when the baby had croup and was up crouping for five straight nights. He couldn't know that she would be the one to get up and sit in the steamy bathroom so he could stay asleep.

Her husband couldn't know that she would hate the sound of someone vomiting so much that he would be the one to handle vomit duty when the babies got sick. He would be the one to handle the smell and the sound, from the time they called it spit up all the way through high school when they called it puke. He would be the one she would kick under the covers when they came home from a late night high school party giggling and he'd hold their hair back and feel no anger, no animus, only love that they were singing the same song they all had sung: "I'll never drink Tequila again."

And yet, in the throes of chemo she was there for him, cleaning up after him. The sound of his gagging must have terrorized her and kept her up at night, but she was there with no sign of displeasure, telling him to get it all out and that he'd feel better in the morning. The same words he used for the girls when they were in high school, and he couldn't help but wonder how she knew those words, those phrases of calm when she'd never experienced an episode like this before.

She'd avoided situations like this her whole life, yet when he was at his lowest, hoping death would come and take him away just to end the never-ending waves, she was there with words of comfort making him believe, somehow, that it *would* be alright and a happy ending would arrive.

But the problem was I waited too long. I didn't ask her in time, and she didn't say yes, to me. Instead she stayed true to her word and moved out to the sound of me telling her that I wasn't ready, but I would be. That it wasn't her, but me. She blew past me and my chair, and the smell of flowers sang to me and lifted my spirits for a moment, only to drop as I begged to the back of her head, not to leave. A face that turned away from me for the final time, a face that I would not see again until I saw the wedding announcement to another man almost two years later.

She looked so happy in the picture, which made me so sad. But not as sad as I felt when I heard about the way her husband died of cancer. How she nursed him for the final two years, how her daughters spoke so well at their father's funeral. How they praised her mother's patience, her commitment, her resolve.

I read all this from my chair in the same apartment where we once lived together. A space where on certain days when the window is open and the breeze is light I can still smell her and the scent from the flowers she planted in the box that still hangs from the window.

# A Pain Called Laura

*There is a pain called Laura and I've reference it many times, mostly in how it feels when an employee quits. It's then I think of her, my 8th grade girlfriend and listening to Billy Joel* The Stranger *album and all that it does to me. I was inspired to write it after reading the publication* Brevity *a journal of concise literary nonfiction. While I saw a fit, they did not.*

THERE IS A PAIN I NAMED FOR HER.

Not out of malice, but because that's what it feels like, to me.

When a certain pain strikes, not in my chest, or my back, but in my gut, it's named for her.

Laura. The one who hurt my heart for the very first time.

Laura, the one I kissed under my blue blazer. I held it over our heads as if it were raining. We were in the back of the bus on the way home from Brent's Bar Mitzvah party.

We kissed and then came up for air. And dove back in again.

We were 12 and I don't know how it started or why it stopped.

But nothing has ever felt that good. And so I feel bad that her name is tied to a feeling that doubles me over in pain.

She was taller than me and everyone made fun when we danced together at the party.

They laughed when they heard I kept a milk crate in my parent's backyard so I could stand on it to reach her lips.

At some point we broke up.

Why did we break up?

Because we were kids.

But it was her idea, that I know.

She wanted more, and I didn't understand what that meant.

But whatever she wanted she found it elsewhere and I learned about pain. A physical pain that happens when nothing is physically wrong, but when your heart has been rejected.

A pain that reminds you of what to avoid.

Like the taste of tequila.

But now I am fifty and the pain in my gut is no less real when I am on the receiving end of an adult betrayal. Employees who quit, children who don't tell the truth and the little white lies that hold marriages together.

I find it amusing that in middle age my deepest pains are named for a girl I hadn't seen in 30 years.

A girl whose kiss and heavy breathing under that polyester jacket plunged my young body into fits of joy. It was a time of so many firsts. Things never again would taste as good.

And so I look her up to tell her of my bemusement. How her name and her body have affected me over these many years. To tell her that she unleashes in me memories as fond as any in my life. Yet, the pain she inflicted, the ending of it, is what my body remembers most viscerally. Or maybe I won't tell her that part.

There is little information I can find about her in the likely places. She is not on social media. She is not on the usual workforce websites.

Her obituary however packs a punch, suggesting she was married twice, with young children and a widower.

Cancer got her at 32.

When I read the obituary I begin to piece together her life and the lives of those I knew back then. I realize she must have divorced and remarried since her children don't have her widowed husband's last name. Her parents have divorced as she is survived by both of them and their new spouses. Her brother never married. She moved across the country.

When I read all this I feel a pain. But it is not the pain named for her. It is not the pain of rejection or cancellation. This is pain of lost youth, of aging, of realizing something was gone and the hope of rediscovering it, is buried.

Realizing the shared memories of sneaking behind her house or running from the neighbors who caught us kissing are now left with me. Alone.

The idea of sharing it with her, or laughing over the moments, are gone. Maybe I would have called and she wouldn't have even remembered me, or the moments I wanted to share. How empty would that have been?

This is not a sadness of youth but the melancholy of middle age. It is not the sharp pain of ended relationships, but the dull emptiness that some things are already dead.

I feel the weight of her loss and am glad I didn't reach her to tell her of the pain. The pain is mine, not hers, the fault is with me, not her. The sweetness of the memories are ours. And now, only mine.

# Blogs and Business Writing

*Throughout Covid there were lots of topics to cover both in my personal blog, which started 10 years ago when we moved to London, and in the Marketresearch.com Blog.*

# Shrinking Turkeys, Expanding Markets

*I love this blog topic, as it is the perfect mix of timeliness and topicality dovetailing with my interests as a writer and market researcher. But I got no bites from any of the major papers so I published it on our blog. Still think it was a perfect piece for someone. I just ran out of time.*

*November 23, 2020*

COVID-19 CAN'T CANCEL THANKSGIVING 2020, BUT IT SURE CAN shrink it.

Banning large gatherings and the fear of infecting grandma have shrunk the Thanksgiving holiday to an almost unrecognizable form.

The CDC has recommended an outdoor version of the holiday where everyone brings their own food, no potluck, buffet or shared utensils.

What does an outdoor Thanksgiving mean to a market researcher?

The turkeys shrink, but the markets grow.

Patio heaters — from fire pit kits to gas radiant patio heaters — are unfindable, with more than $570 million in sales in the US last year. And the 5% compound annual growth rate for propane is exploding.

And while we expect Americans to gorge on the holiday staples without regard to portion-control, ingenuity is making itself known.

Costco shifted from its beloved half sheet cakes to emphasize its smaller 10" round cakes as more suitable for smaller celebrations or just because now you can eat the whole thing yourself.

But this could mean fewer leftovers. While re-usable containers have sealed the deal during Covid, they take a hit as the farmer gods created smaller birds, slicing down on leftovers.

Grocers are shrinking their seafood and appetizer platters as well, which means fewer shrimp, less cocktail sauce, cheese and crackers.

Despite a sluggish restaurant business, the carryout and delivery foodservice are very thankful this season, approaching $380 billion this year. This growth, along with changing hygiene habits, have lifted the disposable packaging market past the $15.5 billion mark.

Historically we took pride in cooking the meal ourselves and claiming it was "homemade," but curbside carryout of family-style meals has lost its stigma.

But even with the growth in carry out, and OPC (other people cooking) Americans are still whipping up family favorites with spices, oils, vinegars and marinades — already worth $4.3 billion in US sales — are hot and spiking as we have more small gatherings which means more cooks in their own kitchens.

Everything from fully-cooked stuffing and gravy to meal kits have heated up past the $4 billion mark as home cooking increased in the pandemic era and families looked for convenient ways to access groceries and explore new types of cuisine.

But even if you are headed over the river and through the woods, you are less likely to bunk in the single bed of your high school bedroom. While hotel occupancy is in the gravy, revenues from lodging services such as rentals, cabins and cottages are bringing home more than $1.5 billion business in the US.

So whether you're eating indoors or out, alone or socially-distanced, carry-out or homemade, Covid-19 can shrink a holiday, but somewhere a market is growing.

# What's Your Story?
# And How To Lead With It

*This topic deserves more than just a short article. I love this topic and want to do more than just write about it. I spent a lot of time working this through in the early part of 2021 and even tried to buy the websites for www.whatsyourstory.com. I think it can be a class or a series of classes, but as of now it's a story and a bigger idea.*

As we emerge from a year of social distancing, distance learning, learning to mask our faces and face our fears, we are approaching a social reengagement such as we've never seen. Since March 2020, the word "connection" has more often referred to Wi-Fi speed than actual human interaction, but this is a moment when learning to tell your story has never been more important.

"What's your story?" That's the only question I ask people when they interview for a job or pitch me a new idea. Everyone has a story, and they need to know it, lead with it and use it. Whether you're interviewing for a job, pitching a new product or going on a date, your story is your power.

On one occasion, a potential salesperson spent his time answering my question by telling me about his sales experience, customer success stories and the way he approaches new clients. He had a fine 20-year sales history, but he wasn't that different from the other candidates we'd been interviewing. When it was over, I walked him to the elevator making small talk and asked if he was from the area.

"No, not really," he said. "I was in a rock band 20 years ago, and we were touring the east coast. We were playing in Georgetown, and we broke up. I didn't have the money to get home, so I started selling."

I stood back for a moment and looked at this man in his late 40s, imagining him rocking the stage on bass.

"That's your story," I told him. It's the lede, the jumping-off point.

**Find your story.**

There are many paths to helping you find your story. Think about:

- A time when you faced a challenge and won.
- A time when you faced a challenge and lost, but learned to win the next time
- Your origin story — this refers to the backstory, often told in comic books, on how characters gained their superpowers — that set you on your path or made you change course.

Knowing your story and being able to tell it in a relatable way is as much about knowing yourself as it is about allowing someone else to know you. Your story is the obvious tale that's often hidden behind your ego. It's your secret weapon, the story that explains who you really are.

**Uncover your true motivations.**

Consider the candidate I once interviewed to be a writer for our healthcare brand.

"What's your story?" I asked.

"I've always been interested in healthcare," he said. "You know, how it helps people."

He was a recent college graduate, and I decided to try to help him explore his interests a little deeper. "Anyone in your family a doctor? Anybody a writer? Was there a movie or television show that really got you interested?"

"My mother died of cancer when I was nine," he said. "I spent a lot of time in hospitals." There it was.

Lots of people end up on their journeys by default; it was a job, and it turned into a career (see reasons for midlife crises). Often, our stories change. The old ones no longer serve us. As we meander into middle age, I marvel at the friends who change careers and leave jobs after 25 years to explore something new.

Your story is your why. Your story immediately tells the listener why you are asking for money, why you are interested in this job or why you are asking for help.

**Be honest, be different.**

How do you tell your story?

- Be memorable: You can't forget this story; it has to be good.
- Don't be afraid to be different: While you might think different equals bad, someone else will see different equals special.
- Be authentic: It's not bragging to talk about yourself in a positive light. It's your story, so tell it.

I recently met with a young entrepreneur who wanted to start a business, and he told me money was important to him. He explained how he and his wife are both the first in their families to finish high school.

I prodded him with questions about money and its importance, and then he dropped: "In our extended family, we've paid for seven funerals in the past two years." Now I understood him. That was his story.

Now go find yours, and have the courage and confidence to lead with it.

# Next Year's Trends
# Are Already Here

*This is a good lesson from MRDC and the human behavior component of market research. It started out with the idea of whether we really change after pandemics. And then it morphed into, we already have.*

ARE WE FUNDAMENTALLY DIFFERENT AFTER MORE THAN A YEAR OF online shopping and social distancing?

This is a key question business leaders are grappling with as we emerge from doing everything differently, from working and cooking, to dressing and living.

As the CEO of a market research business, I know how helpful it can be for corporate executives, startups and chief executives to navigate the years ahead by analyzing how consumers have adjusted during the pandemic and how they might act in the future.

And the verdict is in. I believe the era of coronavirus and quarantines changed consumer behavior and shifted personal spending in ways that will upend how we live, eat and work. While some of these trends will prove to be as fleeting as a New Year's resolution, many are locked in, guaranteed to roil markets this year and beyond.

Nowhere is that more obvious than on the home front, where more pets, fewer births and changing housing preferences will have cascading economic impacts that persist well into the future.

The pandemic pet boom, which brought large numbers of new dogs into households across the country will continue to drive sales in all things pets. Even before the pandemic, 74% of pet owners reported their pets contributed to improvements in their mental health. It was a banner year for pet products, with sales up 9% to $107 billion. Given the average 10-year lifespan for a dog, I believe this sales growth is likely to hold as the new baseline.

And while we were buying furry friends in bulk, there is something we weren't doing: making babies. With 300,000 fewer than average births over the past year, the markets for diapers and baby formula have waned. That may not be much of a hit to large chains, but at a national level, the diaper decline foreshadows cascading changes, including enrollment reductions in daycares, schools and universities, and in time, a reduced workforce supporting an aging population.

As we hunkered down in our homes and began to notice all the nicks and scratches that needed fixing, we made changes, painted rooms, bumped out walls and drove up the associated markets. U.S. consumers used their idle time, vacation funds and increased location flexibility to engage in a wide range of home improvement projects, from adding pools and decks to converting unused spaces into home gyms and offices.

Many of those who could afford a new home bought one, and those purchases will have downstream effects, continuing to drive some markets and sink others. Houses built and designed in 2020 had larger kitchens and more bathrooms, indicative of consumer desires for more space, enhanced privacy and — possibly — the need to accommodate more family members under one roof due to the economic and social dislocations of the pandemic. Consumers also sought more kitchen amenities, as more meals were prepared at home, larger porches and patios to safely entertain and accommodate guests and visitors, ceiling fans to promote air circulation and energy-efficient doors and windows and appliances.

On the other side of the equation, the suburban housing market was blistering hot. As demand grew for getting out of the city and suburban supply vanished, new construction lead the way in a post-pandemic world, causing demand and price hikes for plywood, drywall, siding, roofing materials and such accessories as cabinetry, plumbing fixtures and fittings and flooring materials.

Why are these changes going to persist when Covid-19 is behind us? Because many workers of the world united, and after spending a year at home, they realized they liked it. They didn't miss their lengthy commute times. Now that video chat has proven there is a professional way to communicate from a distance, changes are coming for office space, office furniture, office coffee service and below desk-level business attire.

Companies across these varied industries — which includes multi-national corporations as well as investment banks and consulting firms — should pay attention to where market demand is headed after Covid-19 reshuffled the deck.

Whether planning a new product launch, managing supply chains, expanding into an adjacent market or evaluating an acquisition opportunity, I believe it's crucial that leaders understand what consumers want and how they have changed because of Covid-19.

The end of the pandemic may finally be in sight, but we will be living in a world shaped by Covid-19. I've been taking the pulse of markets for 20 years, and one thing about these future trends is clear — they're already here.

# PPP a Chance to Pause, Plan and Pivot

*I don't have a lot of faith in new government programs, especially if you have to apply for them online. But the PPP plan delivered. And so I wanted to pay homage to how our government can be responsive to the needs of the people and actually come through.*

PPP IS MORE THAN JUST A PAYROLL PROTECTION PROGRAM, IT IS A chance to Pause, Plan and Pivot.

There are any number entrepreneur/investor idioms being thrown around about how to run your business in a crisis: fix the plane while flying is the one being tossed our way.

We are in the midst of the third cataclysmic economic event of our company's life — We raised our first round of financing just weeks before the dot com bust, launched our business nine months before 9/11, and then we purchased a business that sold into the financial markets just months before my CFO came to me and said, "Lehman Brothers can't pay their bill." I told him he was nuts.

Years ago, during one very productive time a member of my team asked: "We feel like Lucy in the chocolate factory, when do we exhale?"

There is never a break, the machine keeps producing candy, the clock keeps ticking, but now we are being given a moment to breathe, sharpen the saw, check the compass, fill the tank.

The PPP program, while not perfect, for many companies is doing exactly what it set out to do: help businesses keep their employees while they reassess and recalibrate in a market that's been deliberately shut down. And I think it's a perfectly good way for the government to act at this moment without precedent.

There are lots of arguments regarding government help for businesses in times of crisis, but what is a business to do? Currently the government requires us, for the public good, to move from our office, set up our employees to work remotely, and try to sell our wares in an economy that we are deliberately contracting.

So the crie de coeur of an entrepreneur is to pivot. Change directions. Make ventilators not cars, hand sanitizer not gin. But not everyone can and so instead of crashing the plane this program says we're gonna give you 8 weeks to pay your employees, bring back those you may have furloughed and figure out how turn to navigate.

The government here is acting as a partner and saying, "Look, we're gonna shrink your market and squeeze some of your customers and maybe even your margins, but instead of figuring this out in mid-flight, we're gonna build a runway for you in the middle of the ocean, let's see what you can do."

When the program was announced we didn't give it much thought because our first instinct is always to turn inward, toward the team, our group of advisors, never to the government.

But we're a midsized company. We're not too big to fail. We're too important to fail.

Too important to our employees. Too important to their families, to their children and their parents and their mortgage-holders and their insurance agents and their car leaseholders and their pets and their co-workers and our office leaseholders and our health insurance company and the hundreds of partners, customers and vendors who rely on the protection of this paycheck, from us.

This plan was conceived to help small companies and their employees. We've been given the space, now it's up to us to get back in the air and soar.

# So Who Are We Now? Remote Work and Its Impact on Company Culture

*The hottest topic during Covid was employee flexibility/happiness and office space. I wrote this piece walking a fine line between what I want as a CEO and what employees want in relation to their work/life balance. When I submitted it some editors wanted it to be more strident in directing people back to the office. But I think demanding a return won't work.*

PARTS OF MY COMPANY WERE ALWAYS HYBRID.

While I was in Washington, DC, there were people scattered from London to Cleveland, Chicago to New York. My business calendar was built around visits to these "offices."

When someone moved to a new state, we often accommodated, but my preference was hiring in places where we paid rent, had desks, walls, cubes and community.

It wasn't the physical space I was attached to, although the addresses are etched in my mind like the phone numbers of childhood friends. It was the people in those places, the cross talk, the meals, the drinks, the ability to get beyond this project or that pipeline. It wasn't the everyday grind that I loved, it was a team of managers scrambling in a Walmart in the Berkshires searching for underwear after getting caught in an April snowstorm, listening to the London office dissect the latest Premier League game as if it were a Shakespearean drama, the "souper bowl" soup contest in Cleveland, the espresso place near the New York office.

I only knew one way to connect with the team and hopefully earn their trust and that was walking across *their* floor, into *their* space, *their* routines. I couldn't imagine who we are without those physical offices.

Then Covid hit and everyone moved home. But in my mind it was a hiatus, a break from the norm to which we would surely return. Then something happened: leases expired, Zoom replaced being in the room where it happened and everyone's sense of time shifted.

Rush hour, traffic, train schedules and weather, those first in the morning brain rushes were no longer the measure of a morning. Like a game of Tetris, blocks of time shifted and could be put in new places, meals and workout schedules were based on a body clock, not a wall clock.

This is the CEO challenge of the year.

There are companies who never moved employees home, and they remain office-centric either because the boss, the business or the customers demanded it. But for those of us who sent everyone home on the Ides of March 2020, the world has changed.

I knew we were firmly in new territory when I went to Cleveland recently and invited everyone to a two-hour, outdoor lunch. It felt like the first day back to school, or a return to summer camp with people hugging, running up to each other, high-fiving..

"I guess Zoom doesn't replace hugs," one person remarked.

We laughed and told stories, shared a meal. At the two-hour mark, though, people headed for the exits. There was little lingering, no thoughts of sticking around and setting up shop in the unused 15,000 square feet.

I can't complain about the results of the business. We've hired good people during the pandemic, trained and onboarded them with success. And the folks who've been here have exceeded their numbers.

But I still feel something is missing.

When I hire people I ask of them for one thing: To Care. I ask them to care about their job, or their co-workers, their customers or the product, but just care, because if they care they will do the right thing when no one is watching. They will be better and they will stay longer.

The world may return to a pre-Covid schedule in 2022, but for those who dispersed everyone home the genie is out of the bottle. For most employees they'll tell you, it's a better life.

So should I make them come back?

When we've called people back to the office they've love it. As long as it's a full house and their co-workers are there. They would rather do a solitary job at their home without the commute and attendant noise. But if they're coming to a place with life, they're all in. They just want to keep some of their well-earned flexibility.

We aren't an assembly line punching out widgets. We are company. A company that is stronger when it is supported by a community. A flexible work environment can work for everyone with the recognition that whatever we are, we are better together.

# Personal Blogs: In a Foreign Land

*When we closed offices and moved everyone home in March 2020 I would write my employees each day with some update about the company or the state of the virus, or the world. So I was already keeping a daily toll on what was happening. I converted it to this.*

Notes to myself: How we got here
April 12, 2020

<u>February 28</u> Corona is taking over, the Virus not the beer.

<u>February 29</u> The market is down 2500 points, a daughter in Florida on Spring Break, another at school in New Orleans preparing for Mardi Gras. My son takes the subway in New York every day to work.

<u>March 2</u> Pete Buttigieg is wins Iowa, or not. Went to see a novelist speak at an overcrowded independent bookstore. She said it feels like we are in a flashback sequence of a pandemic movie when things were normal, and we didn't know what was ahead.

<u>March 3</u> College kids are being recalled from abroad. My business trip to London gets cancelled, not so much for fear of getting sick, but getting stranded.

<u>March 4</u> A friend cancels his 50th birthday party. I wash my hands until they are chapped. I flinch every time I scratch my nose.

<u>March 9</u> I took the subway in New York and the Amtrak home. Someone coughed on the train and everyone got up and left the car.

<u>March 10</u> Biden's deficit in Michigan has turned into a 20-point surplus, how? The market is plunging.

<u>March 11</u> Today everything changed. The market approached bear territory, the World Health Org classified it a Pandemic and Trump is addressing the nation.

I'm supposed to go to the Washington Capitals game tomorrow, but the DC government said there should not be gatherings over 1,000 people. Are they going to cancel?

<u>March 12</u> The headlines scream: The day the sports world stopped

<u>March 14</u> One daughter comes home from school in New Orleans

<u>March 15</u> My College Senior texts me: "They just cancelled graduation"

<u>March 17</u> Today a new term, "shelter in place" where New Yorkers may have to stay where they are.

<u>March</u> 18 They are saying months now. The Treasury Secretary says we could be in for 20% unemployment. They want to send everyone $1000 checks. Biden is sweeping the primaries

We get our son home from New York

<u>March 19</u> Restaurant reservation site OpenTable said reservations in its top cities from Boston to Washington went to zero, as in none, not one.

<u>March</u> 20 Images emerge over China and California with clear skies. Fish in the Venice canals. Car plants close in Detroit. Tax Day gets moved

<u>March 21</u> Once impressive companies like Airbnb, WeWork, and Uber sound like terrible ideas. Sharing offices, using other people's cars and houses?

<u>March 23</u> The Washington Post has a sports page, but no sports section

<u>March 24</u> It feels like the world stopped spinning

<u>March 25</u> The Olympics are postponed

<u>March 26</u>-India and the UK close for 21 days. Three million people in the US file for jobless claims

<u>March 29</u> 2,000 people have died

<u>March 30</u> Here comes the week that matters: Will people pay their rent, their mortgages, their employees?
  They built a field hospital in Central Park

<u>April 1</u> Axios put it perfectly: "At least 835 people died today, the stock market dropped almost 5 percent and it just feels like Wednesday."
  Death toll predictions skyrocket to 100,000-240,000

<u>April 2</u>- I tell my employees we are making salary cuts. The DNC postpones the convention and Wimbledon is cancelled

<u>April 3</u> 6.6 million file for unemployment. A friend's mom dies, and we have Shiva by Zoom

<u>April 6</u> The Queen speaks to calm everyone

<u>April 7</u> The UK Prime Minister goes into intensive care. Some good news, they think the curve is flattening

<u>April 8</u> We have Seder over Zoom. The most oft repeated phrase is not Dayenua, but "I can't hear you"

<u>April 9</u> Bernie Sanders drops out of the Presidential race

<u>April 10</u> Our office landlord writes us notes telling us the office is open and clean, even though we can't go there.

Deaths top 100,000.

# Whither the Handshake?

*Another one where I thought the topic just met the moment perfectly. One of those I sent to the major business publications. I knew it was a good topic because lots of other wrote about this and riffed off it. I published it on Medium.*

So what will really change when we emerge from our houses to the world's altered landscape?

Yes, bowling shoes, buffets and salad bars will become remnants of a time when we could still breath near each other. But one staple of business meetings, interviews and 3-martini lunches, the handshake, is on the chopping block to become a COVID casualty.

During quarantine I've watched commercials and old television shows (Pre-March 1$^{st}$) in horror as people shake hands and then eat a meal. It's suddenly as unpleasant as the endless videos showing a sneeze plume traversing the shelves of a grocery store and smothering the unsuspecting.

There has been some inspired improvisation, but nothing says hello like grabbing someone's hand and making a sawing motion.

It's one of the first formulas of adulthood from my father: Good eye contact plus firm handshake equals good impression.

But what could replace it?

I've seen the boot touch, but it seems to require a bit too much dexterity to become widespread.

There is the Namaste bow, a slight bend at the waist, prayer hands in front, but I'm sure it will have its detractors.

The elbow touch, was demonstrated in all its uncomfortable awkwardness by Joe Biden and Bernie Sanders in their empty debate hall.

The fist bump, as well as the high five are way too close to the handshake, far too much skin contact.

There is the wink which has the advantage of obeying the six feet of social distancing but could get awkward real quick.

They say President Kennedy's discomfort with headwear signaled the demise of the hat business in the United States. But like many things that might be returning we could see a reemergence of the fedora, the panama hat, perhaps the bowler leading to a return of the hat tip.

There's always the curtsy or a bow one might do before a queen, but once we start having differences for men and women, there's lots of judgment.

The end-of-the-performance bow, where the arm unfurls a la Liberace might make a comeback.

A dancing friend suggested parties mirror each other like the Macarena or the Electric Slide. Again this could favor the more gifted or rhythmically inclined.

It's very hard to be bad at the handshake, other than being too soft or too strong which is only then known by the recipient. Being bad at a dance move as you walk up to a table of strangers might not be the entrance one is looking for.

Perhaps the hand clap: You walk up to a table and each of you burst into a round of mutual applause. But when do you stop?

The wave: Not the hand wave, but the wave they do at stadiums. You enter a room of strangers and everyone stands one at a time. Yes it's one-sided but very welcoming. It could encourage people to show up late for meetings.

The hand over heart is a gesture sometimes seen on stage by grateful performers or speakers as a way of thanking their audience. While often confused with cardiac trouble, it might fit the occasion.

But is there anything that could really replace the intimacy of the handshake: the grip, the ability to get close to someone, the chance to really size up a person from the start?

Should the coronavirus linger in a divided country unable to agree on much, perhaps exchanging a hand wipe, a pair of latex

# Graduation Cancelled, Life Postponed, the Kids are Alright

*Jessie graduated from college in the midst of all this. My Alma Mater did a poor job of communicating and trying to make the graduates feel special. So each family did it their own way. Some of her friends dressed it up a bit and had a bigger Zoom call. But the kids didn't seem to mind, they rolled with it better than some of the parents.*

MINE WAS COLD AND RAINY. HERS WAS SUN-DRENCHED.

We drank cheap champagne. Really cheap. She ate expensive Zingermans, and without the wait.

Someone must have had a disposable camera and taken these lovely pictures that show the grayness of the day and the distinct lack of pomp and circumstance. Her day was meticulously documented on Snapchat and Instagram.

This weekend my daughter graduated from the same university I left 31 years ago.

Our speaker was unremarkable. I had to Google the speech to remember who spoke and what he said.

She watched on Zoom. Some friends put together a makeshift commencement speech and everyone worked really hard to make it nice.

Graduation is like New Year's Eve, lots of build up and often, no delivery.

Had we been in Ann Arbor there would have been complaints: it's too hot, it's too cold, this person spoke too long or too short. There was none of that.

The moms made up a poem and read it to the girls. Throughout the weekend everyone got Face-time with the graduate and it was memorable.

There's been an outpouring of concern, lamenting what these kids lost or how they were gypped out of their day.

Rituals are important, they create memories. But sometimes it's the hiccup in the line of rituals that makes them memorable.

The graduation cancellation is a microcosm of the past 7 weeks. The frustrations and disappointments of daily life fade away and the world is a little fresher because we are putting a new stamp on it.

But I am impressed watching this generation surf these waves of disappointment: Interviews on hold, jobs postponed, internships cancelled, plans changed.

In the words of Pete Townsend, "The Kids Are Alright."

There have been tears during these four years. I remember the moment she found out she had gotten in. It was during winter break, when "everyone" had heard the day before. The website kept crashing and then, the tears.

The moment she walked into that dorm, we drove away and I thought we'd never have her home again...Tears, although they were mine.

The ups and downs of life at college are bound to bring successes and disappointments. But the moment she got a text from the University saying "classes are cancelled, go home," must have been the worst.

She texted me and said, "I think I just walked out of my final college class." (tears)

That's the part that stings. Her mindset had been: Two more months of closure, final parties, final trips to Skeeps, final favorite meals, and then someone tells you that you've already had the last one. No more classes, no more crowded bars or pre-games. Those are hard moments for a college kid. For anybody.

But they rolled with it, made it home (more tears), adjusted their lens, found new ways to apply for jobs and finish out their classes. And at the end of the weekend, after all the planning and re-planning the consensus was, they felt loved.

It wasn't what they planned, and that's okay. A great lesson to finish out their college career. "The kids are alright."

# Returning Bugs

*In the Summer of 2021 the cicadas returned to parts of the US after a 17-year slumber. I remember their last go around and I planned for the return. One thing I didn't plan on, how the kids would grow.*

THE CICADAS ARE COMING BACK ON TIME, BUT THE KIDS AREN'T.

Seventeen years ago I wanted to be that guy who took the photo and then re-created it when the kids were older. The one with the foresight that one day things would be different, but I would insert something to make it rhyme.

And so when the cicadas arrived on our windshields in May 2004 I had our fearless daughter (Jessie) pick up the fat bugs, calm her siblings down and pose with them. And then I imagined that in 17 years I would take the picture with bigger people and smaller-looking bugs.

We forget about these things until something jolts us and we realize that it's been 17 years and the bugs are returning and the singing starts anew.

Without notice I slipped into our room where we keep the dusty photo albums and prayed with outsized strength that I would find the evidence with old pictures stuck behind the laminate.

And then I found the year on the spine and turned the pages until I spotted the three shiny photos. I touched them and made that motion one makes nowadays on photos to make it bigger, clearer, as if it were a mobile device. But I couldn't get any closer to the photos, just as I can't get any closer to those kids who later that night probably took baths and got into their pajamas and were tucked into a bed in our house under one roof, with a book and a stuffed animal.

"The cicadas are coming" I told them all in a family group chat.

Seventeen years ago our family group chat was the kitchen table.

"They will be here in May," I wrote with excitement. "Here are the photos from 17 years ago, can't wait to replicate..."

But what I failed to grasp 17 years ago when they were ages 4, 6, and 8 is the same misguidance I'm experiencing now. At 21, 23 and 25 they aren't around for a picture. During the month of May they are at work and away at school. They aren't in the same city or even the same time zone, let alone the same house, bedroom or bath.

Cicadas are grouped into geographic broods. This year's brood will emerge when the soil temperature reaches 64 degrees.

My brood's return is less clear.

And so trillions will soon rise from the ground clicking and chirping to a screeching pitch as they buzz, annoy and procreate.

I could not have imagined 17 years ago that the cicadas would arrive just as we are emerging from our own cocoon.

And so as the song in the backyard begins and I feel the power of nature's rhythm, I am reminded how ours has been disrupted.

If there is one thing we've learned from 2020 it's that making plans is a dangerous game.

I can hear their song in the distance.

A song seventeen years in the making.

But my photo will come.

Maybe not on my schedule. But it will come.

Post Note: Father's Day came June 20, 2021 and they all surprised me by showing up. I had saved a handful of Cicadas in a plastic bag in my desk drawer for the next time I would see them all. So when they showed up for Shabbat Dinner I pulled out the bag and said, "this is our Sunday activity." They all obliged. ➤

# Conclusion

I WILL NOT LOOK BACK ON COVID AND QUARANTINE WITH undiluted pain. There was a lot of progress in there. During the same period that these pieces were written and published I received 273 rejections and 108 no response from various editors.

Like a lot of things, it's a numbers game.

I'm grateful for the time to write, for the acceptances and for the borrowed time with my children, Josh, Jessie and Natalie, to whom this is dedicated. Having the chance to watch them work at their jobs while they worked remotely was a gift.

I am also indebted to the Snooker Club for giving me a place to write. That place is a story, or a setting, for another day.

And of course to Jill, who makes our world go round.

Onward.